COULD IT BE HIM?
DI SALLY PARKER
BOOK THIRTEEN

M A COMLEY

For my rock, my beautiful mother, who is now watching over me. Dementia sucks. Remembering all the good times we shared together.

You took a huge chunk of my heart with you. Love you and will miss you, until we're reunited once more.

ACKNOWLEDGMENTS

Special thanks as always go to @studioenp for their superb cover design expertise.

My heartfelt thanks go to my wonderful editor Emmy and my proofreaders Joseph and Barbara for spotting all the lingering nits.

Thank you also to my amazing ARC Group who help to keep me sane during this process.

To Mary, gone, but never forgotten. I hope you found the peace you were searching for my dear friend. I miss you each and every day.

ALSO BY M A COMLEY

Blind Justice (Novella)
Cruel Justice (Book #1)
Mortal Justice (Novella)
Impeding Justice (Book #2)
Final Justice (Book #3)
Foul Justice (Book #4)
Guaranteed Justice (Book #5)
Ultimate Justice (Book #6)
Virtual Justice (Book #7)
Hostile Justice (Book #8)
Tortured Justice (Book #9)
Rough Justice (Book #10)
Dubious Justice (Book #11)
Calculated Justice (Book #12)
Twisted Justice (Book #13)
Justice at Christmas (Short Story)
Prime Justice (Book #14)
Heroic Justice (Book #15)
Shameful Justice (Book #16)
Immoral Justice (Book #17)
Toxic Justice (Book #18)
Overdue Justice (Book #19)
Unfair Justice (a 10,000 word short story)
Irrational Justice (a 10,000 word short story)
Seeking Justice (a 15,000 word novella)

Caring For Justice (a 24,000 word novella)
Savage Justice (a 17,000 word novella)
Justice at Christmas #2 (a 15,000 word novella)
Gone in Seconds (Justice Again series #1)
Ultimate Dilemma (Justice Again series #2)
Shot of Silence (Justice Again series #3)
Taste of Fury (Justice Again series #4)
Crying Shame (Justice Again series #5)
To Die For (DI Sam Cobbs #1)
To Silence Them (DI Sam Cobbs #2)
To Make Them Pay (DI Sam Cobbs #3)
To Prove Fatal (DI Sam Cobbs #4)
To Condemn Them (DI Sam Cobbs #5)
To Punish Them (DI Sam Cobbs #6)
To Entice Them (DI Sam Cobbs #7)
To Control Them (DI Sam Cobbs #8)
To Endanger Lives (DI Sam Cobbs #9)
To Hold Responsible (DI Sam Cobbs #10)
To Catch a Killer (DI Sam Cobbs #11)
To Believe The Truth (DI Sam Cobbs #12)
Forever Watching You (DI Miranda Carr thriller)
Wrong Place (DI Sally Parker thriller #1)
No Hiding Place (DI Sally Parker thriller #2)
Cold Case (DI Sally Parker thriller#3)
Deadly Encounter (DI Sally Parker thriller #4)
Lost Innocence (DI Sally Parker thriller #5)
Goodbye My Precious Child (DI Sally Parker #6)
The Missing Wife (DI Sally Parker #7)

Truth or Dare (DI Sally Parker #8)
Where Did She Go? (DI Sally Parker #9)
Sinner (DI Sally Parker #10)
The Good Die Young (DI Sally Parker #11)
Coping Without You (DI Sally Parker #12)
Could It Be Him (DI Sally Parker #13)
Frozen In Time (DI Sally Parker #14)
Web of Deceit (DI Sally Parker Novella with Tara Lyons)
The Missing Children (DI Kayli Bright #1)
Killer On The Run (DI Kayli Bright #2)
Hidden Agenda (DI Kayli Bright #3)
Murderous Betrayal (Kayli Bright #4)
Dying Breath (Kayli Bright #5)
Taken (DI Kayli Bright #6)
The Hostage Takers (DI Kayli Bright Novella)
No Right to Kill (DI Sara Ramsey #1)
Killer Blow (DI Sara Ramsey #2)
The Dead Can't Speak (DI Sara Ramsey #3)
Deluded (DI Sara Ramsey #4)
The Murder Pact (DI Sara Ramsey #5)
Twisted Revenge (DI Sara Ramsey #6)
The Lies She Told (DI Sara Ramsey #7)
For The Love Of… (DI Sara Ramsey #8)
Run for Your Life (DI Sara Ramsey #9)
Cold Mercy (DI Sara Ramsey #10)
Sign of Evil (DI Sara Ramsey #11)
Indefensible (DI Sara Ramsey #12)
Locked Away (DI Sara Ramsey #13)

I Can See You (DI Sara Ramsey #14)
The Kill List (DI Sara Ramsey #15)
Crossing The Line (DI Sara Ramsey #16)
Time to Kill (DI Sara Ramsey #17)
Deadly Passion (DI Sara Ramsey #18)
Son of the Dead (DI Sara Ramsey #19)
Evil Intent (DI Sara Ramsey #20)
The Games People Play (DI Sara Ramsey #21)
Revenge Streak (DI Sara Ramsey #22)
Seeking Retribution (DI Sara Ramsey #23)
Gone… But Where? (DI Sara Ramscy #24)
I Know The Truth (A Psychological thriller)
She's Gone (A psychological thriller)
Shattered Lives (A psychological thriller)
Evil In Disguise – a novel based on True events
Deadly Act (Hero series novella)
Torn Apart (Hero series #1)
End Result (Hero series #2)
In Plain Sight (Hero Series #3)
Double Jeopardy (Hero Series #4)
Criminal Actions (Hero Series #5)
Regrets Mean Nothing (Hero series #6)
Prowlers (Di Hero Series #7)
Sole Intention (Intention series #1)
Grave Intention (Intention series #2)
Devious Intention (Intention #3)
Cozy mysteries
Murder at the Wedding

Murder at the Hotel

Murder by the Sea

Death on the Coast

Death By Association

Merry Widow (A Lorne Simpkins short story)

It's A Dog's Life (A Lorne Simpkins short story)

A Time To Heal (A Sweet Romance)

A Time For Change (A Sweet Romance)

High Spirits

The Temptation series (Romantic Suspense/New Adult Novellas)

Past Temptation

Lost Temptation

Clever Deception (co-written by Linda S Prather)

Tragic Deception (co-written by Linda S Prather)

Sinful Deception (co-written by Linda S Prather)

PROLOGUE

ive years earlier

FEELING out of his depth and with the rhythm of the music pounding in his head, Denis followed his mates, Ray and Vince, through the nightclub. It was heaving. Denis had never been here before; going on the prowl for women wasn't really his thing. Why would it be when he had a good woman, one of the best, waiting for him at home?

He had been dragged along this evening, kicking and screaming, because Ray was desperate to get a new woman after being dumped by his long-term partner who had kicked him out of the house she owned. Now he was living permanently, or so it would seem, in Vince's spare room. How long that would last was anybody's guess.

They joined the long queue at the bar.

Ray was crafty; he worked his way through to the front after spotting a mate behind the bar. "Mark, over here. How are you doing?"

"All right, Ray. Haven't seen you in here for a while. On the pull, are you? I heard your missus kicked you out last week."

Ray shrugged. "Her loss, not mine. I was getting bored with her anyway. So yeah, I'm here on the pull. Three whiskies when you've got a mo, mate."

"Coming right up. Normal or the extra-special variety?"

Ray glanced over his shoulder. "Normal will do, thanks."

The barman delivered the drinks and took Ray's money and the tip he gave him and wished him luck for the evening.

Ray handed the drinks around. "Shall we get closer to the dance floor?"

"If we have to," Denis complained, still regretting his decision to tag along this evening. His head no longer felt like it belonged to him, and that was only after a couple of pints and a few whiskies, and the night was still young yet. He groaned internally at the prospect of having to watch Ray treat the women like they were at a cattle market, ripe for the taking.

Ray swooped in on every available woman he reckoned was in her thirties and got knocked back every time until one woman appeared to appreciate his full-on advances and he went back to the bar to top up their drinks.

"Want another, gents?"

Denis slipped a hand over his glass. "I'm fine, you sort yourselves out. She seems nice."

"Yeah, she's called Sonia. That's all I know about her at the moment. I'll see you later, guys. Have fun."

And that was the last Denis and Vince saw of him for the rest of their stay at the club. Vince gave the impression he was as bored as Denis.

"Want to call it a night soon, mate?" Denis asked.

"Yeah, this isn't really my thing at all. I'll just nip to the loo. Can you watch my drink for me?"

"Sure."

Vince headed off to the toilets near the entrance, and Denis stood there, looking like a lemon, holding two glasses in his hands. He moved off to the side of the thoroughfare to the bar and bumped into a bloke.

"Sorry, pal. It's difficult to know where to stand around here."

"You spilt my drink, tosser. What are you going to do about it?"

"Nothing. I apologised. You've still got three-quarters of a pint there, you should be good for the rest of the night."

"It was full. That means you just robbed me of a quarter of a pint and I want to know what you're going to do about it to put things right."

"I said nothing." Denis was resolute and stood his ground.

Vince appeared alongside Denis and whispered in his ear, "Is everything all right here?"

"Yeah, it's sorted."

Denis turned and walked away. He could sense the narked fella's gaze boring into the back of his head but was determined not to look back.

That's all I need, a confrontation with a goon who is eager for a fight to top off this sorry evening. All I want now is to get home and snuggle up with my wife. Why the heck did I agree to come here this evening?

"Are you all right, Den?"

He smiled and nodded. "Nothing another glass of whisky wouldn't put right. Want one?"

"Not for me. I haven't changed my mind; I think I'm going to head off after this one, if that's okay with you?"

"I was thinking the same. We've accomplished our aim tonight, there's no need for either of us to hang around any longer in a place where we can't think straight."

Vince nodded. "If this is what old age feels like…"

They both laughed, and Denis followed Vince through the crowd back to the main entrance. They downed the rest of their drinks and left the nightclub. Vince lived on the opposite side of town to Denis, so he jumped in the first available cab. Rather than spend money he didn't really have on a taxi, Denis decided the fresh air would help to sober him up and set off on foot.

He noticed his feet weren't performing the way they usually did and decided to have a rest for a minute or two on a wall outside a terraced house a few hundred feet from the club. He watched the couples spill out of the club and walk past, obviously on a promise, judging by some conversations he'd overheard. Amused by their antics, he began his journey once more and even decided to go through the park, a shortcut he often took when he decided to walk home from the pub around the corner. It was well lit, so he couldn't see there being a problem taking that route. He wasn't sure he had the legs to stagger the long way home anyway.

The large gates were up ahead of him. The path was narrow and wound its way through the trees and shrubs. He smiled, remembering the last time he'd come through here arm in arm with Frances; it had been on their anniversary a couple of months ago. She hadn't wanted to go out for a meal, all she needed was a nice stroll around the park before going home to watch a movie whilst having a cuddle on the sofa. That had been music to his ears to hear her say that, as funds were short at the time.

Deep in thought, he neglected to hear what was going on behind him. That changed when he received a whack to the head. He staggered a few steps, lost his footing and ended up veering off the path into one of the thorny shrubs. Confused, he lay there, hampered not only by the whack he'd received but also by the drinks he'd consumed during the evening.

The combination rendered him incapable of righting himself or even protecting himself from further attack.

Too late, he was wrenched from the shrub by two strong arms.

"You fucking weasel. All of this could have been avoided, if only you had topped up my pint." The man sneered and laughed at the same time, making his mouth twist into an ugly mess of malevolence.

"All right, mate, you've had your fun. Time to move on now and let things lie."

"Says you. You're not the one whose bloody drink got wasted, are ya? No, I'm going to punish you good and proper. Blokes like you need to be taught a lesson they're not likely to forget in a hurry."

Denis gulped, and the man laughed then pushed him ahead of him. He had one hand on his shoulder and the other holding his belt, keeping Denis upright.

"Where are we going?"

"Button it. You'll find out soon enough. Keep walking. How much have you drunk tonight?"

"Enough."

"How much?" the goon repeated.

"Five or six. I lost count after the third pint at the pub."

"Where did your friends go?"

"One is still in the club and the other got a taxi home. There's no need to help me like this, pal, I can manage the rest of the way home by myself. I've done it dozens of times before."

"Good for you. It's my pleasure, and you can stop calling me your pal or mate, I'm anything but…"

Denis puffed out his cheeks, not liking where this predicament was leading him. His wayward thoughts weren't helping him come up with a solution to get himself out of the fix he was in either. "I'll pay for an extra pint of beer, if that will make you happy, ma…"

"Like I give a shit about my pint now. No, I've got better things on my mind right now, and they're all to do with the punishment I'm going to mete out to you."

Denis stopped walking, but the man bumped into the back of him and urged him to carry on.

"Don't stop now, not when things are about to get interesting, *mate*."

Just by his tone he was making his intentions clear and putting the shits up Denis.

"Wait, there's got to be something I can do to make things right between us. What happened at the club was a missstake," he pleaded, his words now affected by the drink he'd consumed, or was that fear talking?

"Shit happens, right? You should have thought about that back there. I gave you the opportunity to put things right, but you messed up. You need to own your *missstake* now, *Pal*."

"I've got money in my wallet, have it. You could probably buy ten pints with what's in there. That'll make things right between us, won't it?"

Take that and I'll have nothing left until the end of the month, you fucking moron.

"I'd say it's too late for that. You had your chance and messed it up. I'm not one for giving someone a second chance, not these days. Life's too short, ain't it? It makes life interesting. Correction, it makes my life interesting when dickheads like you screw up. I'll let you into a secret: I enjoy it all the more when people are remorseful for their actions. It doesn't make me think twice about punishing them, though. Oh no, once you've done the dirty on me, no one gets a second chance."

"What? You can't go through life holding on to that attitude. Where is that going to lead you, eh?"

The man laughed. "You'll find out soon enough, don't worry about that."

Denis tried to look around him. The rest of the park was empty. If he cried out for help now, he had a feeling that whatever this guy had in store for him could get a lot worse, so he decided to go with the flow for now in the hope that the adrenaline rushing through him would help sober him up.

The bloke kept guiding him round the winding path to the entrance on the other side. There, Denis was hoping a passerby would come to his assistance, but again, the street was empty. A sinking feeling swept over him. They came to a stop beside a Subaru. The man clobbered him again, knocking him out.

When Denis woke up, they were in a field. He felt cold and realised the man had stripped him down to his boxer shorts. "What the fuck is going on here? Hey, you're not one of them, are you?"

The man tipped back his head and laughed. "No, you're safe in that respect. You're not my type."

Relief swept over Denis, but only for a moment or two. "So, what are you going to do to me then?"

The man leaned in closer and tapped the large machete in the palm of his right hand. "Let me think... Ah yes, this." He swung the weapon, and it sliced through Denis' ankle.

The movement happened so swiftly that Denis didn't get a chance to try and stop it. The pain was excruciating. He screamed and stared at his right foot, lying detached on the grass. The blood gushing out of his wound made his head swim. "What the fuck are you doing?"

"When are you going to learn to keep that mouth of yours shut?"

"I... umm... I... you can't go around lobbing people's limbs off like this."

"Can't I? Watch me!" He grappled with Denis' right arm and extended it, then he swiped the machete across the wrist. The blade chopped through the joint with ease.

Denis watched on in horror as his hand fell to the ground beside him. He screamed out again, but what was the use? There was no one around to hear him. That was this guy's intention, wasn't it? "Please, no more, don't do this. All I did was spill your drink and this is how you punish me?"

"Not only did you spill my drink, but you disrespected me in the process. I don't take kindly to fuckers like you thinking you're better than me."

"What? I didn't. I apologised at the time. How did I disrespect you? This is all wrong, you're bang out of order. You need to get me to the hospital. Maybe they'll be able to sew my limbs back on, make me whole again."

The man laughed. "Whatever. I ain't finished with you yet."

The machete came at him again and swiped a deep wound in his stomach. Denis stared at the open wound. The pain hadn't registered yet, there was a delayed reaction, and he couldn't figure out why.

"No scream this time? You must be getting used to it. Good, time for more."

Denis stared at the man, who had obviously lost his marbles, as blow after blow ripped his body to shreds. His life flashed before his eyes, and they closed for the final time.

CHAPTER 1

"How long before you complete each of the houses?" Sally asked her husband.

Simon smiled. "By the end of next week, if everything goes according to plan. Your dad is overseeing the snagging list on one property, the smaller terrace. Tony is in charge of the second property, the detached house on the outskirts of Attleborough, and that leaves me to deal with the flat conversion which has been a thorn in my side for weeks now."

"Oh, you never said. What's been the problem?"

"I didn't want to burden you with it, you have enough to contend with on a daily basis as it is."

Sally moved closer and lifted her head for a kiss. Simon planted a quick peck on her lips.

"A problem shared and all that. What problems have you encountered?"

"The building inspector was a pain towards the end, and then there were a couple of safety issues we had to overcome. It's all done now, so the renovations are back on track."

"I can't believe you've managed to get all three properties

finished at around the same time. You guys must be delighted with how the business is progressing."

"You could say that. We make a great team. I think it has given Tony and your dad a new lease of life."

"I'm so pleased, for all of you. Who would have thought the business would be thriving this much after only a few short years?"

"I know. I do have to pinch myself now and again. Anyway, enough about business, or should I say my business, how are things going at work?"

"Same old, same old. We cleared the backlog of cases last month. We're hoping the Super doesn't start making the cuts he threatened to make a while back."

"I'll keep my fingers crossed for you. Do you have time for breakfast?"

"You bet. What did you have in mind? Nothing too heavy for me."

"Shall I knock you up some pancakes?"

Sally closed her eyes and moaned. "I think I've died and gone to Heaven. Do you have the time?"

"Sure. Do you want to give Lorne a shout, see if she and Tony want to join us?"

"Now, that's a great idea." She picked up her mobile and rang her partner. "Hi, it's me. Have you eaten yet?"

"You caught me putting cereal in a bowl, why?"

"Put it back and come and join us. The invitation is open to Tony as well. Simon is knocking up pancakes for us. I'm sure I can rustle up some bacon as well."

"God, really? We'd love to join you. See you in five."

Sally ended the call with a beaming smile. "They're on their way. They decided cereals wasn't a good enough start to the day. Shall I put some bacon under the grill?"

"That'd be great. The mixture is made. I'll start making

them now and we can keep them warm in the oven until the others get here."

A few minutes later, Lorne and Tony entered the back door and hugged them both.

"This is a lovely surprise, thanks for the invite," Tony said. "Anything we can do to help?"

"Get the cutlery out and lay the table," Simon replied.

The four of them had been friends for a few years now, the men not as long as Sally and Lorne, but they had become inseparable since Lorne and Tony had left London and moved in to run the kennels next door. Working together only seemed to strengthen their friendship, which was a blessing.

They enjoyed the filling breakfast and stimulating conversation then went their separate ways. Sally always gave Lorne a lift to work when she could; it not only saved on fuel but passed the time during the boring journey, too.

"Simon said they're hoping to complete three properties by the end of next week. Isn't that amazing?"

"It is. I hear that two of the properties have already sold before they've had a chance to market them," Lorne replied.

"Blimey, he never got around to telling me that news, he was too busy singing Tony's and my dad's praises."

"It's great the business has been such a success, especially as the market has been turned upside down lately."

"I suppose quality always shines through in the end. By now, all the estate agents in the area know their standards are impeccable, so they tend to have a list of buyers lined up before the properties are half completed. It doesn't always pay off, but nine times out of ten it does. I'm so proud of them, of what they've achieved over the years."

"Me, too. I couldn't be prouder. It's such a thrill knowing that we made the right move coming up here to Norfolk. I just wish we got to see more of Charlie. That's the one downside to moving away from London."

"Hey, she visits when she can. Any news about her getting another fella yet?"

"No, I think she's steering clear of men at the moment, and who could blame her? I believe she's keen to rise up the ranks quickly and only sees men as getting in her way."

"I don't blame her. Any chance you can persuade her to settle up here with you?"

"I'm working on it. Especially after the backlash the Met has received from the press lately."

"Has she ever come across any misogynistic behaviour?"

"No, not that she's been willing to share. She's lucky in that respect, working alongside Katy. It might have been a different story if her partner was male."

"Too true." Sally's mobile rang. "Here we go, that has an ominous ring about it."

"You're nuts, it's probably Simon wondering what you want for dinner this evening."

Sally laughed and answered the phone. "DI Sally Parker, how may I help?"

"It's me, Pauline. Are you free?"

"Hi, Pauline, yes, Lorne and I are just on our way in to work. What's up?"

"Can you join me?"

"Depends. Where are you?"

"At present, I'm standing in a field out near Acle, staring at the remains of a corpse that was discovered by the farmer a few hours ago. Interested?"

"We're on our way. Can you send us a pin with your location?"

"Sending it through now. See you soon."

"Can you deal with that, Lorne, and insert the location into the satnav?"

"Consider it done. Great start to the week, eh?"

"That's one way of putting it. Still, if it keeps the Super off our backs for a while, it can't be all bad."

Lorne entered the location, and within seconds the satnav had calculated the route. "I think I know where it is, roughly."

Sally glanced sideways quickly and then returned her gaze to the traffic ahead of her. "We should be there within ten minutes, unless this lot grinds to a halt in the meantime."

THEY ARRIVED at the scene later than anticipated due to a small prang ahead of them. Sally had stopped to check if the drivers and passengers were okay while Lorne rang the station to request the assistance of a patrol car. The drivers were quite nonchalant about the accident, so Sally decided to leave them to it and continue the journey to the scene.

Pauline was standing by her van, her arms crossed, tapping her foot. "It's about bloody time. I expected you here sooner than this."

Sally walked towards her. "All right, wind your neck in. An accident happened not long after I spoke to you. We had to hang around and sort it out before we could get on the road again."

"Sorry, I wasn't aware of that."

"So you should be. I'm not in the habit of giving out false information to pathologists."

"All right, there's no need to go on. Let's call a truce now before either of us says something derogatory."

"Derogatory? Me? Christ, I know we're still trying to get to know one another, but you're way off the mark if you believe I would ever be that rude to a fellow professional."

Lorne nudged Sally in the back, and it was then that she realised she'd gone too far with her response.

Pauline's head dropped, and her cheeks coloured up. Within seconds, she murmured an apology. "I'm sorry. Of course, you're right, I overstepped the mark in our new professional relationship. Can you ever forgive me?"

Sally took a step forward, encroaching into the pathologist's personal space. "Hey, let's forget about it. Put it down to experience; we were both out of line."

Lorne applauded, startling both Sally and Pauline. The three of them laughed, and the awkwardness was soon forgotten.

"Can we get back to the job in hand?" Sally smiled. "Do you need us to get dressed for the occasion?"

"Always a good idea, whether the corpse is associated to a cold case or not," Pauline replied.

Sally and Lorne collected a set of Tyvek overalls and shoe covers each from the back of Pauline's van at her insistence, as if making up for any insults she had dished out. Once they were suited and booted, they joined Pauline at the muddy graveside of the skeleton.

"Male or female? Or is that a silly question at this stage of the process?" Sally asked.

"Don't hold me to this, but my initial findings are telling me that we're looking at a male."

"And the farmer was by himself when he found him?"

"That's right. He was in the process of digging a trench to put new pipework in, and as you can see for yourselves, this is what he discovered."

"How long ago?"

"A couple of hours, although we've only been on site for the past forty-five minutes, therefore, pre-empting your next question about any relevant evidence, no, we haven't had a chance to look for anything as yet. You know how hectic everything is once we arrive at a scene of this nature. One of my first priorities was giving you a call."

"Which I appreciate. Shall we leave you to it and have a word with the farmer?"

Pauline shrugged. "It's up to you. I'm about to start my examination now that everyone is here. The farmer is over there, sitting in his tractor, waiting for you to interview him. Fair warning for you, he was in a bit of a state when I spoke with him earlier."

"Understandable. Thanks for the heads-up. We'll be back soon."

"Good luck. Right, now where was I before I was rudely interrupted?" Pauline asked her second-in-command, dismissing them.

"Come back, Simon, all is forgiven, right?" Lorne whispered as they walked away.

Sally chuckled, but discreetly, in case Pauline thought they were saying anything derogatory about her as they were leaving. "She's an unknown quantity at the moment, isn't she? One day I think we're getting on great together and then she either says or does something that flips that idea on its head."

"I suppose we still need to give her time to settle in. What is she, thirtyish?"

"I don't know her well enough to acquire any personal details, yet."

"She'll come around to our way of thinking, sooner or later."

"I hope so. Our job is challenging enough as it is without the need for us to show up at a crime scene, only to walk around on eggshells."

Lorne sighed. "I'll give you that one. Maybe we should drag her out for a night out, that might help her get to know us a bit better."

"Good idea. The next barbecue we have, her name will be at the top of the list."

"I'll remind you."

"Thanks." Sally glanced ahead of her at the way the farmer was holding his head. "This was a tough find for him. I think we're going to need to tread carefully with this one. Can you take down any necessary notes?"

"Don't worry, it's all sorted. He does seem a bit down. I suppose I would feel the same if I'd dug up a body on my land."

"God, can you imagine? We've both got huge gardens… no, I refuse to go there. Let's focus on the task in hand for now."

"Yeah, let's not go down that route. If I mentioned this conversation to Tony, he'd be expecting me to hire some of that thermal imaging equipment to go over every blade of grass we own."

"He wouldn't! He's not that anal, is he?"

"Trust me, he would."

"Don't make me laugh, I'm trying hard to keep a straight face here." Sally coughed to clear her throat.

They were a couple of feet from the tractor when the farmer finally saw them approaching his vehicle.

He offered up a weak smile and a brief wave and climbed down from the tractor's cab. "Hello, I've been expecting you. I'm Eric Chalmers. Is this going to take long? I'm a bit shaken up, you see, and I'm eager to get back to the farmhouse for a much-needed cuppa with an added shot of the hard stuff to calm my nerves."

"We can relocate to the farmhouse if you'd rather do that? Whatever suits you, however, we'd need to interview you a bit later rather than waste another suit." Sally pointed at the paper ensemble she was wearing.

He nodded. "I get you, here's fine. My needs don't matter in the grand scheme of things, do they?"

"Of course they do. It must have been a shock for you to discover the body."

"That's a gross understatement. I'm just thankful I had a pacemaker fitted last year because I don't think I'd be here otherwise, the shape my old ticker was in before the op."

"Sorry to hear that. Do you feel up to speaking with us now?"

"Yes, I think the sooner the better."

"My partner here will be taking notes throughout, if that's okay with you?"

"Do what you need to do. I fear I'm not going to be able to tell you much."

"There's no pressure from us, take your time." He nodded and Sally continued, "what time did you discover the body?"

"I left the farmhouse just as the sun was rising."

"Sorry, I'm not generally up before six-thirty."

"I got washed and dressed at four-forty-five."

"Did you come down here right away?"

"After shoving a piece of toast and a cup of tea down my throat. I like to set myself up properly for the day. None of this nipping home after an hour's work for a cooked breakfast like in my father's day."

"Have you owned the property long?"

"Around four years. Although my family have been farming in Norfolk for decades. Buying this farm, which is twice the size of the one my father ran in his day, was supposed to bring us in more money. Ha, that's a bloody laugh."

Sally frowned. "I'm assuming the opposite is true. I would have thought that was a given if it was twice the size of your previous one."

He puffed out his cheeks and shook his head. "Gone are the days you see farmers driving around in brand-new Range

Rovers. Nowadays we have to contend with climate change and all that it brings to the party. Droughts, floods, you name it, it's a constant battle, I can tell you. Tougher than any time I've ever known through the decades. My father says he's never seen the like of it, and he's been farming for over sixty years, and his father did the same before him. Our hands are tied when the damned weather is out of our control. Yes, we can change what crops we grow to combat the hotter weather they predict for the summer months, but it's getting that crop to start growing that's the problem. Still, that's none of your concern, sorry."

"You don't have to apologise. I just don't know what to say in response. I know a lot of us are complaining about the prices at the checkouts right now, but it's this side of things that the general public aren't fully aware of, and we should be."

"Precisely. Which is why the government need to be doing more to help us. But again, that's another issue and doesn't really cover why you're here today. I can tell you, when I first found the body, I thought my eyes were playing tricks on me. If I hadn't jumped down from my tractor to ensure the channel was deep enough, I would be none the wiser and probably would have scattered the bones within another couple of digs."

"So it was a test patch, is that what you're telling us?"

"Exactly." He ran a hand through his longish hair that was greying at the temples. "Such a shock. An unbelievable shock that knocked the wind out of my sails. Never in my wildest dreams have I ever encountered something as… horrendous, I suppose you'd say. I've never seen a skeleton before, not a real one. I can remember we had a plastic one in the science lab at school, but this is nothing in comparison. All I keep thinking about is this person's family and how the hell he or she came to be buried here."

COULD IT BE HIM?

"All valid questions that we're hoping the pathologist will be able to answer over the coming days or possibly weeks."

"Weeks? Goodness me. I asked the pathologist if she had any idea how long the body had been buried, and she struggled to answer me."

"It's pretty complex, the testing that needs to be done to obtain a definitive answer. Pathologists generally prefer not to commit themselves at this stage of the proceedings. You told us you've owned the farm for the past four years. Can you tell us who worked this land before you?"

"Old Tom Jenkins, but he's dead now. Died a few months before the farm was put on the market. I got the property for a knockdown price because his kids wanted shot of the place and quickly. I believe they shared the money between the three of them, two boys and one girl. None of them were interested in taking on the place to run as their own. I can understand why after reading the last few years' accounts. Tom didn't have a clue about running a farm as a business, and don't get me started on what a state the farmhouse was in when I took over. The place had to be gutted from top to bottom, even fumigated before I moved in. I lived in a caravan on the drive for the first year or so, much to my wife's disgust. She never wanted us to buy the farm in the first place. Told me it would be a money pit. I had to admit she was right after the first couple of months, and now this. I rang her earlier, she's beside herself, ready to pack her bags and leave me. I reckon this is one step too far for her now."

"I'm sorry to hear that. Maybe she'll calm down once you're able to speak to her in person."

"I doubt it. She told me not to rush back to the farmhouse because she needed to contemplate where our relationship was going." His hands rose and slammed against his thighs. "As if all of this is my fault. It's just a huge nail in a coffin that was ready… sorry, I should stop right there, given the circumstances."

"Don't worry, feel free to speak openly and honestly with us."

"Thanks. What a bloody mess, to have you lot show up here like this. I'm struggling to make any sense of it. I can't help wondering who the bones belong to. That's not too macabre, is it?"

"No, I would say it's normal. I think I would be racking my brains to uncover the truth if I were in your shoes."

"Wait, you don't think I have anything to do with this, do you?"

Sally raised a hand. "That's not what I was insinuating at all, far from it."

"How long has the body been down there? I suppose that should be your first question, shouldn't it? And not one I'm able to answer, I can assure you."

"The pathologist will let us know as soon as she's carried out a thorough examination of the bones back at the lab. As soon as those details are to hand, we might have to come back and interview you again."

"I get that. But I'm telling you now, this has nothing to do with me. If I'd done away with someone, I wouldn't bury them on my own ground and dig them up years later, would I? Furthermore, do you think I would have reported it to you guys? No, I can categorically say I wouldn't have done that. Not all farmers are thick, despite the general consensus of opinion."

Sally liked this man. It was refreshing to speak with someone who came across as honest and sincere. Her heart went out to him regarding the turmoil he was living through at this time. "I hear you. Don't worry, we won't be coming down heavily on you, Mr Chalmers. We'll let you get on now.

I just need to take a few personal details first, before we let you go."

"Such as?"

"Your address and your wife's name, and also a contact number for yourself. Can I leave that with you, Lorne?"

Lorne nodded, and Sally slipped away from the conversation. She came to a stop, halfway between Lorne and Pauline to survey her surroundings. As in other parts of Norfolk, this area was reasonably flat. She noticed the burial site was quite close to a hedgerow and moved towards it. It led to the main road, possibly the same road they'd driven down to get to the scene, even though they had entered the field off to the side once they'd spotted the other vehicles. There was a small lay-by close to where the corpse had been found.

"Penny for them?" Lorne came to stand beside her.

Sally pointed out the obvious. "A lay-by directly in front of the grave."

"But no entrance on this side of the field, not that I can see."

"Absolutely. Unless that has changed over the years. Maybe we should ask Eric if he's made any alterations to the hedgerow since he's owned the farm."

"I'll do it now while it's still fresh in our minds." Lorne trotted back to the farmer who, by now, had started up his tractor. He killed the engine, and Lorne asked him the question then returned to Sally. "Nope, he says every entrance is still the same as it was when he bought the farm."

"Well, that answers that problem then. So, the person who buried the body either entered the field the same way we did, or they were already on site in the first place."

"Are you suggesting the previous farmer has something to do with this?"

"Possibly, but he's dead now. Unless…"

"One of his kids buried the body here," Lorne completed the sentence for her.

"Anything is possible, and nothing can be ruled out at this stage."

"True enough. Want me to ring the station, get the guys doing the necessary research into the family?"

"You read my mind."

Lorne removed her phone from her pocket and made the call while Sally continued to walk along the hedgerow. Lorne caught up with her a few moments later.

"All actioned. What's our next step?"

"Go back to Pauline, see what she's discovered, if anything, then we'll head back to the station and start digging. We'll need to check the Missing Persons' list as well."

Lorne waved her hand from side to side. "Might be too early for that if we haven't got a definitive answer as to how long the body has been buried."

"You're right. We'll put that on hold for now."

They wandered back to the makeshift grave to find a pensive Pauline staring at the corpse.

"Anything wrong?" Sally asked. She crouched beside her, her suit rustling noisily.

"I'm just studying the remains in situ. The guys have excavated the soil further, giving us better access to the corpse now. Don't quote me on this, because you know nothing is a hundred percent definite this early in the proceedings."

"Go on, we're all ears. Anything you can give us will be a bonus to start our investigation."

"Okay, hold on to your hats, bearing in mind that the information I give now may alter later on."

Sally rolled her eyes. "Okay, I won't hold you to anything, I promise. What are you seeing?"

"His lower legs, both the tibia and fibula, are broken on

both. The right hand and right foot are both missing. That's all I have for you at present."

"Thanks, that's something at least. Could the broken bones be stress fractures, possibly due to the way the body was buried?"

Pauline halted her with a raised hand. "Let's not get carried away with the questions just yet. That's as much as I'm willing to share at this time."

"I'll back off then. Umm… one more obvious question, if I may?"

Pauline side-glanced her. "And that is?"

"The foot and the hand, could they still be in the grave, underneath the body? Is it possible they might have become detached from the skeleton over time?"

"It's a possibility. We can't rule anything out during my preliminary assessment."

"That's good enough for me. When do you think you're likely to be able to give us more information about the remains?"

"Remind me how long that proverbial piece of string is again, Inspector? There are too many variables for us to consider."

"Which are?"

"You're aware that cold cases have their place in the queue and don't get priority over new cases, therefore, erring on the side of caution, in case another fatality comes my way soon, I would say if we have a clear run at it, I should have something positive for you by the end of the working day tomorrow, so first thing Wednesday morning at the latest."

"Can we join you for the PM?"

Pauline shrugged and frowned. "Is there any specific reason you'd like to attend when you've never requested to be at a PM I've conducted before?"

"I just thought it would be interesting to see how things progress, that's all."

"You can tag along, I have no objections to that at all."

"What time shall we be there?"

Pauline raised an eyebrow. "Are you tugging on that piece of string again, expecting me to answer it now?"

Sally grimaced. "Roughly?"

"We're going to be here for a few hours yet. These things need to be carried out carefully. The best I can offer is to give you a call once we're on the way back to the lab."

"I'll settle for that. Do you need us here any longer?"

"No, you're free to go."

Sally smiled and rose to her feet and stretched out her legs that had become numb from crouching. She and Lorne walked back to the car.

"I sense this one isn't going to be easy to solve," Sally said.

"I agree, not from the information we've gathered so far. I think we're going to need to sit on our hands for a while until we attend the PM, and even then, going on past experience, I doubt if we'll be able to jump right in and get things started."

"Christ, hark at you, ever the optimist, not."

Lorne laughed. "I'm just saying we need to be prepared for this one. I think it's going to drive us to distraction from the outset."

"Hey, I'm always open to suggestions, you know that."

"When I have any, I'll be sure to let you know."

They stripped off their suits and deposited them in the black bag one of the techs had tied to the gate.

Then Sally began the drive back to the station, she and Lorne both lost in their own thoughts.

"I do love a challenge, but even I have my limits."

"I sense we're going to need to be patient with this one, Sal."

"I think you're right."

"At least we've had a decent breakfast to set us up for the day."

BACK AT THE STATION, and with the daily post now dealt with, Sally rejoined her team. "I know it's early days yet, but do you have anything for me?"

Lorne nodded. "I checked the electoral roll, went back a number of years and found the names of the children of Tom Jenkins. Mark and Jason Jenkins, and there was a daughter called Lucinda. I've checked the system and I'm having trouble locating them as still living in the area."

"Frustrating. It might be worth calling the neighbouring farms. Maybe one of the other farmers can tell us where the children are living now."

"I'll get on it right away," Lorne said.

"Anything else?"

Joanna lifted her hand, and Sally crossed the room to see what she had to tell her.

"I took the liberty of searching through the archives, see if anything came up, and I found a story in the local newspaper about Mark Jenkins. He was eighteen at the time and was found guilty of drink-driving. He put several children in hospital after his car mounted a pavement."

"Shocking. Anyone seriously injured?"

"Thankfully not. He was given a suspended sentence and took flack for it from a couple of the children's parents."

"Hmm... so that might be the reason we can no longer find him in the area. Hang on, what about probate? Can we find out who was the solicitor who dealt with the father's death? They'll probably be able to fill in the blanks for us."

"Leave it with me, boss."

And that was all they could do at this stage, until Sally

attended the post-mortem. With every member of her team hard at it, she decided to nip out to the baker's to buy lunch for all of them. During her trip, she received the call she'd been waiting for from Pauline, who requested her company at four that afternoon. Aware of how long the PM could possibly take, Sally rang Simon to warn him she might be late home.

His phone rang and rang. She was about to give up when he finally answered.

"Sorry, busy as ever going through the final details with the site manager. How has your day been?"

"You don't have to apologise. I was ringing to prewarn you I might be late tonight."

"Oh, any particular reason?"

"We've taken on another cold case. A body was found buried in a field out at Acle, and we're due at the mortuary to attend the PM at four."

"Ah, I see. That'll take a few hours to complete. Shall I knock up an omelette when you get home?"

"Don't worry about me, just sort yourself out for dinner tonight. I'll be home as soon as I can. Hope all goes well at your end for the rest of the day."

"Thanks. By the look of things, we're going to need more than luck if we want to pull this one off by the deadline."

"Maybe it would be better to postpone it and let the other two go to market rather than rush things."

"I'll take your advice on board. I must fly now. Enjoy the rest of your day, or was that the wrong thing to say?"

Sally laughed. "Perhaps. See you later. Love you."

"Love you, too." Simon ended the call before she did.

There was something in his tone that alerted her to the amount of stress he'd put himself under in order to get all three properties completed. The off-licence was next to the baker's; she'd drop in there and get a nice bottle of wine to add to his collection in the hope that would cheer him up.

WITH LUNCH out of the way, Sally went over the information the rest of the team had cobbled together. "So, Lucinda married a Christian Monty and is now living in Hereford. I'll see if I can get in touch with a colleague down there, ask them to pop round and see her rather than contact her over the phone. What about her two brothers?"

Lorne showed Sally her notes. "As far as I can tell, they both moved over to the Lake District, close to Whitehaven. I've found the address for Mark, perhaps Jason lives with him."

"If not, either Lucinda or Mark should be able to tell us. Again, I'll get in touch with the team up there and get the ball rolling. We'll leave here at around three-fifteen, Lorne, just in case the traffic is bad. I suggest you give Tony a call to warn him you're likely to be late. I've already rung Simon; he was a tad stressed."

"That's not like Simon. Perhaps they've taken on too much with the three renovations all completing around the same time."

"I said as much to Simon. Still, if they have to delay one then so be it. It's not like it's a life-or-death decision they need to make, is it?"

"Christ, I hope you didn't say that to him?"

Sally chuckled. "Grant me with some sense. Want a coffee?"

"Thanks. I'll give Tony a call."

Sally made coffees for the team and delivered them to her colleagues then joined Lorne again. "Everything hunky dory with Tony?"

"Yeah, I think so. I picked up on a little stress in his tone, but he's not likely to admit to it. Hopefully things will work out for the best for both of them soon."

"If nothing else, it will be a learning curve for them not to stretch themselves to the limits next time."

"Where would the fun be in that?" Lorne said.

"It would make more sense to me. Why put themselves under pressure just for the sake of it? Oh God, enough about them. I hate waiting around, staring at the clock all the time."

"Umm... why are you then? Aren't there a couple of calls you could be making?"

"I can take a hint, and yes, you're right. I'll be in my office if you need me." Sally took her coffee and the notes Lorne had given her and returned to her office but left the door open.

She rang the station in Hereford first and spoke with her female counterpart down there, Sara Ramsey.

"Hi, I'm DI Sally Parker from the Norfolk Constabulary. Do you have five minutes to have a chat?"

"I do, actually. You've caught me having a sneaky cuppa in my office. What can I do for you?"

"Ditto. We're delving into a cold case that came our way today and we're trying to trace the previous owners of the property. Our research is telling us that Lucinda Monty now lives in Hereford."

"And you'd like me to visit her rather than you contact her over the phone, is that it?"

"Spot on. Would you mind?"

"Of course, things are a bit slack here today. I can nip out now to have a chat with her. Do you have her address?"

"Ah, that's the problem, I don't. Any chance you can run her through the system at your end?"

"Will do. You'd better give me a lowdown on what you've found and what type of information you want out of her when I track her down."

"The corpse was found buried in a field on the farm that her father used to own. He passed away a few years ago, so we can't interview him about what we've discovered, therefore, we need to question the children, see what they know about the body, if anything. I know it's a long shot, but I think it would be better to speak to the three kids in person, see what their reactions are rather than call them."

"I agree, a face-to-face meeting is always advisable in these types of circumstances. Okay, leave it with me for a day or two. I'll get back to you as soon as I can."

"I really appreciate it, thanks, Sara. Hey, I'll willingly return the favour one day, if the need ever arises."

"That's great to know. I'll be in touch soon."

"Thanks. Bye for now." Sally ended the call and immediately rang the police station up in Workington. She was put through to their most experienced officer who also happened to be another female inspector.

"DI Sam Cobbs, how can I help?"

"Hi, thanks for taking my call. I'm DI Sally Parker of the Norfolk Constabulary and I have a tiny favour to ask of you."

"Go on, surprise me. What do you need?"

Sally went through the details again with Sam and paused with her fingers crossed as she waited for her response.

"Hey, I'm a little snowed under at the moment. I can't promise anything, but I might be able to track the brothers down and call round to see them in the next day or two, if that will do?"

"That would be great. I can't give you their address, sorry. I just know they're now living in the Whitehaven area."

"Don't worry, if they're in the area my team and I will do what we can to find them. We don't tend to get many cold cases to work on; what's it like to deal with them?"

"It can be super frustrating, searching for the evidence and interviewing often reluctant witnesses or members of the family. But it's satisfying when we wrap up a case and can give the victim the burial they deserve."

"I bet. Nice chatting with you, Sally. I promise to get back to you soon."

"Thanks, Sam. Good luck."

Lorne appeared in the doorway, and Sally beckoned her into the room.

"It's out of our hands now. I've spoken to two female inspectors, one in Hereford and the other in Cumbria, who are both willing to do the legwork for us regarding the siblings."

"Result, that'll be a load off your mind."

"You could say that. Are you almost ready to go? I think we should get on the road five minutes earlier, just in case the traffic is bad. I wouldn't want Pauline to have a go at us for being late."

"Yeah, I agree. If we make a move now, we should miss the schools kicking out."

CHAPTER 2

In the end, they made it to the mortuary by the skin of their teeth, much to Pauline's disgust.

"I told you what time I was going to commence the PM, you could have at least had the decency to have arrived with five minutes to spare."

"Believe me, we set off in plenty of time but what we hadn't anticipated was the roadworks they've just put in place on the A595."

"Perhaps you should download an app which informs you of the relevant roadworks in your area. I have it on mine and I'm rarely held up," Pauline scolded her.

"I'll bear that in mind," Sally said and chewed on the inside of her mouth to prevent her from saying what she really wanted to say.

"Come on then, get cracking. You should be all togged up by now. I'll be waiting in the theatre for you both. Don't be too long. I want to get out of here sometime tonight, even if you don't."

"We'll be two minutes."

Pauline pushed through the swing doors and left Sally seething.

"Christ, do you think she suffers from acrophobia, sitting on that damn high horse of hers?"

Lorne laughed. "She's winding you up most of the time, and you allow her to get away with it. It must be a pathologist's trait. I had the same with Jacques in the beginning. He soon changed his ways once he realised I wasn't rising to his antics."

"Yeah, and look where that led the two of you."

Lorne's cheeks coloured up, and Sally rubbed her arm. "Sorry, that was uncalled for. I didn't mean to upset you. I know how much you loved him."

"I did. I still think of him now and again. Still feel guilty for getting him involved."

"It wasn't your fault. When are you going to get your head around that? Hey, these things are sent to try us. Think of it this way, if Jacques were still with us today, I doubt if you'd be married to Tony."

"I know. Ifs and maybes never did anyone any good, did they? We'd better get a move on if we want to avoid another tongue-lashing from Petulant Pauline."

Sally sniggered. "Oh God, you've nailed it with the nickname, that is so apt for her."

They fastened each other's gown and slipped on their half wellies then made their way down the hallway. Pauline was standing next to the corpse, her arms folded, staring at them as they took up their positions on the other side of the remains.

"Finally, now we can begin."

Sally found it fascinating listening to Pauline describe the victim and the state the remains were in.

"Here you can see several marks on a couple of the ribs. I believe these were probably made by a large blade, possibly the same instrument that chopped off the man's foot and hand."

"I don't suppose you can tell us if the wounds were inflicted before or after the man's death, can you?" Sally asked.

"Not possible, sorry." Pauline removed a tooth from the mouth of the victim and popped it into a tube. "We'll need that for DNA purposes."

"Can you give us any indication of how long the body was buried?"

"I can give you a rough idea. We're testing the soil et cetera from around the body; that will give us a clearer indication, but the results might take a day or two to materialise. For now, I'm willing to put my neck on the line and tell you that I believe the man has been dead anything between four and six years."

"At least that gives us something to work with, thanks. What about his height? If you can give us that we can search the missing persons' files, see what comes of that."

Pauline asked Lorne to hold the end of the measure and then walked the length of the skeleton. "One point eight-eight metres or six feet two in old money." Pauline smiled.

Lorne released the measure and jotted down the information in her notebook.

"Great, at least it will help us whittle down the possible suspects on the missing persons' list. I don't suppose you can give us an approximate age for him?" Sally studied the remains and predicted it would be difficult to do, judging by the state it was in, but then she wasn't a professional pathologist.

"Let me see if I can tell by what's going on in his mouth." Pauline fell quiet for the next few moments while she examined the victim's teeth. "Hmm… okay, don't hold me to this, but I would say between thirty and thirty-five. No, let's err on the side of caution and put him between thirty and forty. Will that do?"

"Perfect, another detail that will help us. Is there anything else you can tell us?"

"He's got a couple of crowns, upper sixth and lower fourth."

"Great job. Thanks, Pauline." Sally glanced up at the clock on the wall. It was close to eight already. "Do you need us for anything else?"

"No, I think we're done here now."

"I have a quick question, if that's all right?" Lorne asked.

Pauline nodded.

"The missing hand and foot, were they found at the burial site today?"

"That's a negative. I believe the killer probably took them as some form of trophy, either that or he was killed elsewhere and transferred to the field and the killer forgot to take the other limbs with him. Pure conjecture on my part, of course."

"Seems logical either way," Sally agreed. "Okay, we're going to make a move. Will you send me your report ASAP?"

"As always. Enjoy the rest of your evening, ladies."

"Will you be long?" Sally asked, guilt pricking her.

"Another hour or so. I'll chip away at a few bones, take as many samples as I can in order to get a more in-depth report for you. But don't let me stand in the way of you leaving early." Pauline winked and smiled.

"We won't. Have fun," Sally replied, then she and Lorne left the theatre.

"I'm glad she gave us permission to leave, I was flagging in there," Lorne said as they stripped off their protective gowns and boots.

"Me, too. It's been a long day, and I'm eager to get home to see how Simon is."

Sally dropped Lorne off outside her house and continued the journey deep in thought about the victim. *Who are you? And how did you die? More to the point, who killed you?*

She drew into the drive of the mansion house she shared with her husband at the same time as Simon. Ever the gentleman, he jumped out of his car and opened the door for her. She stepped out and straight into his welcoming arms.

"I take it someone needs a hug more than I do tonight."

He kissed her and smiled. "You're not wrong. I've ordered a Chinese, I hope that's okay? It should be here in twenty minutes or so."

"Wonderful. That'll give us time to get out of our work clothes and into something more comfortable."

He wiggled his eyebrows. "Really?"

Sally tutted. "Get your mind out of the gutter. I'm starving. Any funny business going through that mind of yours will have to wait until later."

"Spoilsport."

They made their way to the front door.

"Damn, hang on, I forgot Dex, he's in the car."

"Bless him. I'll get changed and take him for a walk, unless you've already let him have a run."

"Ah, time kind of got away from me this afternoon, sorry."

"No problem."

Dex came hurtling towards Sally, almost knocking her off her feet.

"Have a quick wee, and we'll get you sorted soon, boy, I promise."

Dex was a good, super-intelligent dog who understood most conversations going on around him. He ran to the edge of the drive and cocked his leg up a flowering weigela shrub that Sally's parents had bought and planted for them a couple of years ago.

"Not ideal, boy. Come on, scallywag, in you get."

Simon cracked a smile and shook his head.

Despite being dead on her feet, Sally changed into her jeans and her fleece jumper, knowing that the fresh air and a stroll down by the river would do both her and Dex the world of good. "I won't be long. I'll heat mine up when I get back."

She put Dex's harness on, and they set off. The evening song of the birds in the nearby woodland added to the ambience of her walk with her favourite four-legged friend. She let Dex off the lead once they were away from the main road, and he immediately ran into the water for a paddle.

"I bet that feels good after being cooped up in the car all afternoon, eh, boy?"

Dex barked and dipped his head under the water and plucked out a large stone that he deposited on the riverbank.

"You nutter."

Sally threw a few smaller stones in the water, but he ignored them and went on to rescue yet more large stones which he placed in a neat row on the bank. Job completed, he looked up at her and barked excitedly.

"Come on, you, let's go home. You must be hungry after your heroic exploits."

He responded by jumping back into the river and retrieving another couple of large stones. She grabbed the handle on his harness to prevent him from diving in again.

"Monkey, I said we're going home now."

She attached the lead, and they walked back to the house only to see the takeaway van pulling out of the drive.

"Good timing, eh, chum?"

Simon waved and went inside. He threw the dog towel out of the front door and put his thumb up.

"Thanks," she shouted.

After ensuring Dex was reasonably dry, she let him in,

hung up his harness and removed her shoes, then headed into the kitchen to find Simon pouring a glass of red wine. "Damn, I've got a present for you in the car. I won't be long."

"Hey, it can wait, your dinner will get cold."

"I'll be two ticks. You carry on." She dashed out to the car and returned with the special bottle of wine she'd bought him.

"What the…? I haven't forgotten our anniversary, have I?"

"No. Nothing like that. Can't I treat my husband now and again?"

"I'm shocked. This is perfect for my collection." He stood and gave her a kiss. "I don't deserve you."

"I know." She smiled, her heart swelling at the pure glee etched into his features. "I recognised how stressed you were today, so I thought I'd do something nice for you to cheer you up."

"You're amazing but you know that already."

She stared at her bulging plate. "This looks delicious, but there's far too much here for me."

"Leave what you don't want, I'm sure I'll have room for it. With all the hassle I had to contend with today, I somehow missed out on lunch." He removed the batter from one of his chicken balls, blew on it and gave it to Dex, who was lying under the table. "Here you go, boy. I have some making up to do where you're concerned, too, don't I?"

"Oi, not at the table, and definitely not at the beginning of your meal. You know I can't abide dogs begging."

He cringed. "Sorry, my mistake. Do you want to tell me about the body that was discovered today?"

"Can we leave it until after we've eaten? I've only just rid myself of the ghastly image I was confronted with during the PM today. Why don't you tell me about your day instead?"

"It was just busier than normal. You know how hectic the final days can be before a property goes to market. Times that by three, and you can work out for yourself the amount of stress I'm under."

"So why do it? Why didn't you stagger the completion dates on the three properties?"

He pulled a face at her. "Because I'm not as smart as you. Tony, your father and I all agreed that we could pull it off. What we hadn't anticipated was four men ringing in sick and the alterations the council expected us to make as we raced towards the final hurdle."

"Is it all sorted now?"

"It should be tomorrow."

"Good."

They tucked into their Chinese, but Sally only managed to eat half her meal. Defeated, she handed her plate to Simon.

"You've barely touched it, are you sure?"

"If I eat any more, I'll burst. You finish that, and I'll tidy up the kitchen, then we can go through to the lounge and have a chat." She glanced up at the clock; it was already nine-fifteen. *Where has the day gone?*

She left the table, fed Dex his dinner and threw the takeaway cartons in the bin, then took her drink through to the lounge. Simon finished his meal, rinsed the plates and sat beside her on the cosy sofa.

"Now are you going to tell me about this new case of yours?"

"There's not much to tell really. Pauline rang me first thing this morning, asked me to join her at a farm out at Acle. The farmer had been digging a trench and discovered the remains of a male."

"I bet that was a shock for him."

"And some. Poor bloke was a wreck when Lorne and I showed up."

"Any idea who the victim was? How long the body had been buried?"

"No to who the victim is, and Pauline reckons he might have been buried between four and six years ago."

"Ouch. I suppose it'll be a case of you and your team searching through the missing persons' files from around that time to make an identification. Anything else found in the grave along with the victim?"

"Nothing else in the grave, and yes, my team are already on it. I've also been trying to trace the previous farmer's children. He passed away about four years ago. The children are now living in Hereford and Cumbria, so I had to contact a couple of colleagues in the relevant areas, ask them to do the legwork for me. It's not ideal, but it'll save a lot of time."

"I hope the other officers are as diligent as my darling wife."

She held up her crossed fingers and took a sip of her wine. "So do I. Oh, yes, there was something else that might be significant to the investigation."

Simon frowned and tilted his head. "And that is?"

"The victim was missing his right hand and right foot."

Her husband stared at her for a while before he asked, "Anything else, or is that too hard to say at this stage?"

"During the PM, Pauline confirmed the man had two broken legs and there were a few nicks on his ribs as if a large blade had been used. Why?"

"Lower legs?"

Sally nodded.

"I seem to remember a serial killer from a few years ago who went around chopping limbs off people, in particular their right foot and right hand."

Sally sat up. "Really? It wasn't one of my cases, otherwise I would have remembered it."

"No, not one of yours. The perpetrator was caught and banged up for life. It's definitely worth you delving into, though. The corpse found today might have been one of his victims. Let me mull it over for a while, see if I can come up with the killer's name."

"It would be great if you could. Do you want a top-up?"

He smiled and gave her his glass. "Have I ever been known to turn down another glass of fine wine?"

"Yeah, it was a silly question on my part." Sally left the lounge, her adrenaline pumping and her mind racing. There was something right at the back of her mind, itching to come forward. She picked up her phone from the kitchen table where she'd left it and Googled the case.

"Bob Wallace has been in prison for the past four years. He killed seven men and removed the right foot and hand of each of his victims. The limbs were later found at his house along with other remains that had yet to be identified," she said to herself.

"What's the holdup? A man could die of thirstation, you know." Simon placed his arms around her waist and peered over her shoulder. "Now how did I know you'd be out here Googling it?"

"Sorry, you know what I'm like. Is this the case you were referring to?"

He released his arms and moved to stand in front of her. "Yes, that's the one. Wallace. He was a cold, calculated character from what I can remember. I seem to recall, he led the SIO a merry dance with his shenanigans. Told him about several places to dig for bodies and they all turned out to be false. He always requested to be at the scene and laughed when they didn't find anything at the sites. He was an evil bastard in the court as well. I was on the stand giving my evidence and I kept a close eye on his reaction. He would look over at the victims' families and sit there smirking, goading them. A few of the family members complained about his behaviour which only made him worse. In the end, several family members had to be escorted from the courtroom. Again, he just sat there, laughing, mocking the others."

"No remorse shown for his behaviour then. That's sickening. Can't stand people like that. I hope he gets what's coming to him inside."

"I doubt it. He'll more than likely be in good company these days with the number of serial killers there are banged up. It wouldn't surprise me if they didn't spend most of their days comparing notes, evil fuckers."

Sally could tell Simon was getting riled up, he wasn't usually the type to swear. She rubbed his arm. "Okay, let's not let this spoil what is left of our evening."

"Too late. God, it's all coming back to me now. The tension surrounding the cases, the inspector in charge, can't recollect his name now, he was well out of his depth. I think the case affected him that much that he was off sick for a few months with stress. I don't think he ever came back. Might be worth you checking it out."

"If he struggled during the investigation, I doubt if he gave the case his all then."

Simon nodded. "That's what I'm thinking. There could be further victims out there. Wallace never did make a full confession as to how many lives he'd taken. May he rot in bloody Hell. Twisted shits like that should be banged up for life and never see the light of day again. It's obvious they haven't got a decent bone in their bodies, so why should they ever be set free to walk amongst us again?"

"I totally agree. Serial killers are in a league of their own. Most of them come across as intelligent so-and-sos, but there's something missing that prevents them from living a normal existence. If I had my way, I'd send them all to a deserted island and let them kill each other."

Simon laughed. "That's my girl."

He topped up the wine himself, and Sally speed-read the rest of the article then stared at Wallace's photo.

"Here, shall we take this up to bed?"

"You go, I'll let Dex out and follow you up."

Glasses in hand, he went to walk past her but paused and leaned in for a kiss. "Don't be long."

"I promise."

Dex was sitting by her side and whimpered.

"All right, boy. Out you go." She let him out of the back door and removed his evening treat from the tub in the corner. Dex trotted through the open door a few minutes later and sat for his treat. She checked his feet weren't wet, locked the back door, switched off the lights downstairs, then ascended the stairs, her mind still racing with the possibility that she might have already solved the case, and on the first day, too. That rarely happened.

CHAPTER 3

Sally spent most of the night tossing and turning and was glad when the alarm finally went off at seven. She shot out of bed and had showered and dried her hair by the time Simon had prised his eyes open.

He stretched and smiled. "Good morning. You're full of energy today. Wouldn't it have anything to do with what happened when we came to bed last night, would it?"

Sally sauntered over to the bed and pecked him on the nose. "Of course it would. I'm going to ring Lorne, see if she fancies starting early today. If not, I'll tell her to make her own way in this morning. Do you fancy some breakfast?"

"Blimey, you're offering to make breakfast for me? I must have made a lasting impression last night."

"Stop teasing and answer the question."

"Don't worry about me, I'll sort myself out with some cereal later."

"Fine. I'll just have some cereal, see to Dex and shoot off. Have a good day. I hope it turns out to be better than the one you had yesterday."

"Thanks. Good luck with your research today. I think you're going to nail this investigation in record time."

She kissed him again. "With your help. Love you."

"Love you more," he called after her as she ran down the stairs full of vigour compared to how she had finished work the previous evening.

Sally rang Lorne, knowing that her partner would be up since the crack of dawn to see to the dogs boarding with her at the kennels. "Hey, it's me. I know it's early, but I want to set off earlier than normal if you're up for it?"

"How come? Is everything all right?"

"Yep, great. Are you up for it or are you busy seeing to the dogs?"

"No, I've just finished the morning chores. I need to jump in the shower. I can be ready in twenty minutes if that's any good for you?"

"Wonderful, I'll pick you up then. I'm just going to have some cereal now. Have you already eaten?"

"Yes, I was starving and had my breakfast at six-thirty. See you soon."

Sally ended the call and tore around the kitchen, seeing to Dex and pouring her cereal and milk into a bowl at the same time. She consumed her breakfast but couldn't tell you what she ate or drank because her mind was elsewhere. She did, however, keep a close eye on the clock and was ready to leave eighteen minutes later.

"See you tonight," she called up to Simon. She urged Dex to go back upstairs. "Go on, where's Daddy? Go have a cuddle, boy."

Simon responded sleepily that he would make them something special for dinner if the day went according to plan.

She left the house and sprinted to her car. Lorne was

standing outside her gate, waiting for her when Sally drew up.

"Sorry to be a pain in the bum, I've hardly slept all night and I'm desperate to get on with things this morning."

"Not a problem. Are you all right? You seem a little agitated."

"Not really. I was telling Simon about the case last night, and he shocked me with a revelation."

"Go on, or is your intention to keep me dangling?"

Sally laughed. "No, sorry. My head is still spinning from the news he delivered."

"Which was?"

Sally removed her phone from her jacket pocket, opened it with her passcode and handed the article to Lorne. Then she put her foot down and headed towards the station.

"What am I looking at? A serial killer called Bob Wallace was arrested and held accountable for seven murders and…?"

"Keep reading."

Lorne read on, and moments later, she gasped. "Jesus, you think the body we discovered yesterday is another one of his victims, don't you?"

"The question is, don't you? After reading that?"

"Well, it would be tough to rule out considering the part about the limbs. It says here that he was sentenced and put away four years ago."

"It also says that further body parts were found at the house after he was arrested. We need to find out what they were and if some of those limbs match the skeleton that was dug up yesterday."

"Christ, this is unbelievable. Wait, how did you hear about this fucker?"

"Simon, he worked the case. Told me the officer in charge had to take sick leave because of the stress he was under."

"Wow, what are the chances of that happening?"

"Right? Simon also told me the killer is a right shithead; he kept leading the SIO on a merry dance, telling him where he'd buried bodies, insisted he should be there during the dig and laughed when they failed to find anything."

"Perverted knobhead. No wonder the SIO had to take time off. Any idea who was in charge of the case?"

"I can't remember reading it in the article. That should be the first thing we check on today. See if he's still in the Force or if he retired on medical grounds."

"I'll get on it right away. Shit, I don't think I've ever come across this before in all my years in the Force."

"No, me neither. You know what it means, don't you?"

Lorne winced and replied, "That we'll have to pay this bastard a visit in prison."

"Yeah, the thing is, I don't want to go in there all guns blazing. We need to take a step back and assess things properly first."

"I agree. I suppose the first thing we'd need to do is match the limbs to the skeleton. They'll still be lying around somewhere, won't they?"

"I'm presuming the lab will still have them, but who knows after all this time?"

"Like I said, this isn't something I've come across in my thirty years of being a copper."

"We'll do the necessary first thing, and then I'll give Pauline a call, see what insights she has on this."

"Good idea."

The rest of the journey was spent discussing the crimes Bob Wallace had committed, and Sally filled Lorne in on how the bastard had behaved in front of the families during the court case.

"Christ, and I can just imagine how bitter and twisted he's become since being inside. It's not going to be an easy task paying him a visit."

"What are you saying, that you think I should take a male officer with me?"

"No, not at all. Although, it might be worth considering."

Sally sighed. "I'm not so sure. Simon seems to believe that the SIO back in the day was male, so two females showing up shouldn't make a difference."

"I hear you, plus all his victims were male."

"There you go then. That's settled, we'll both go."

Lorne chuckled. "As if I had a choice in the matter anyway."

Sally faced her and grinned. She drew into the station car park and slotted into her designated space.

The desk sergeant, Pat Sullivan, checked his watch the second they entered the main reception area. "Bloody hell, I'm shocked to see you here so early, the pair of you."

"Cheeky sod," Sally retorted. "We come in early when we see fit, it's not our fault you're never around to witness it."

"Touché," he shouted as they slipped through the security door.

"What do you want me to check on first?" Lorne asked.

"Can you sort out the file for me? See what's on the system, and we'll go from there. I'll tackle the necessary post, get it out of the way early, and then I'll be free for the rest of the day. Depending on what you find out, I'll give Pauline a call at around ten. That should give her enough time to get sorted at her end."

HALF AN HOUR LATER, Lorne knocked on her door.

"Come in, take a seat. Bear with me, I have one more email to respond to and then I'm all yours."

"As you wish."

Sally typed up a brief response to an urgent email from head office regarding several cases they had worked on the previous year. "Bloody HO do my head in at times. Someone needs to get a life up there and let us get on with our work. They're always needing some minor details about a previous case. Drives me nuts."

Lorne grinned. "Rather you than me. That sort of enquiry used to be the bane of my life. I can't say I miss being in charge."

"I don't blame you."

Sally bashed the Enter button to send the email. "There, job done, until the next batch of mindless enquiries lands in my inbox. What have you managed to find out, if anything?"

"The SIO was Larry Andrews, and he retired four years ago because of stress."

"Great, we'll need to try and find him, see if he's up to speaking with us about the case."

Lorne's mouth twisted. "I wouldn't be too thrilled about it if I'd left the Force, but I'll try and locate him. I also took the liberty of ringing the Norwich prison and spoke to the new governor up there who said he'd be willing to let us visit this afternoon at around three."

"Blimey, you are on the ball, aren't you? Okay, that's good to know, and what if we can't make it, did he offer an alternative?"

"It's this afternoon or not until next week as they have officials coming to see how he's settling in. He'd prefer not to have any other distractions while the visits are taking place."

"Fair enough. This afternoon it is then. Anything else?"

"I'm still digging. It's a large file because of the number of victims concerned but it's still lacking in content. Not something you or I would be happy to sign off on."

"Great. Maybe that was the fault of the SIO who took over. Who was that?"

"Andrew's DCI, Mark Connors. Sadly, he passed away from lung cancer last year after thirty-five years of service."

"Bummer. Things are stacking up against us, not sure I like that. I'm going to give Pauline a call earlier than I said. I might be able to catch her before she starts her first PM, if she has any on the table, so to speak."

Lorne smiled and left the room. She said good morning to a couple of members of the team who had arrived in her absence. Sally noted the time was eight-fifty-five and wondered if she was chancing her arm calling Pauline this early. She decided to take a punt.

"Hi, Pauline, I'm glad I've caught you, it's DI Sally Parker. Can you talk?"

"I can, briefly. I have a PM I need to be getting on with ASAP. What can I do for you, and no, that's not giving you permission to start hounding me about the results of your PM. I told you to expect it Wednesday morning. That suggestion hasn't changed."

"It's in connection with that, if you can hear me out."

"Go on then, get on with it. My time is valuable, as you know."

"As is mine," Sally snapped back unintentionally. "We believe we know who the killer is."

"What? How? Who?"

"Hold your horses and I'll tell you."

"I'm waiting, not so patiently."

"I can tell it's not your strongest attribute. Actually, it was Simon who came up with the answer after dinner last night. I mentioned the skeleton we'd discovered yesterday."

"Wait just a minute... Are you supposed to take your work home with you like that?"

"I... umm..."

"It's okay, I'm teasing you. You're bound to talk shop, even if Simon is now retired from the profession."

"You bugger. Are you going to shut up long enough for me to tell you what he said or not?"

"Your wish is my command. The floor is all yours, I promise."

"That remains to be seen. As I was saying before I was rudely interrupted…"

Pauline tutted.

Sally chose to ignore her and carried on. "I mentioned the injuries the victim had suffered, and it jogged his memory about a case he had worked on around four to five years ago. The suspect, Bob Wallace, was sentenced to life for killing seven men. The other interesting fact was that all the victims had broken lower legs and each of their right feet and right hands had been removed."

"Whoa, stone the crows. What the heck? So, are we putting the skeleton we found yesterday down as one of Wallace's victims?"

"Possibly, it would be daft not to because of the timeframe. Here's the thing, and where your help will come into play… when they raided the killer's home, they found all the limbs of the victims plus some extra ones. Before you ask, that's as much as I know right now. I haven't got a clue how many other limbs were discovered. Would you be able to check for me? I don't know what the protocol is about storing excess limbs; would they still be at the lab?"

"I can definitely look into that for you. If the limbs didn't match the victims to do with the original investigation they should have been stored somewhere, in the likelihood that more victims might be found in the future."

"Which was what I thought. Can I leave that with you?"

"Absolutely. As soon as I've got a spare moment, I'll do some research and ask the rest of the team, who have been here longer than me, if they can remember the case. If we can find the extra limbs maybe we can match a hand and foot to the remains we found yesterday."

"Exactly. Lorne and I have an appointment at the prison

this afternoon. The new governor has given us permission to interview the killer."

"Wow, go you. Glad things are going at full steam ahead on this one."

"I do my best where possible. Of course, it depends on what evidence and facts come my way."

"I'm sensing that's a dig, am I right?"

"Nope, merely stating facts as usual."

"I'll get back to you later this afternoon. I have to go and cut up a body now."

"Them's the breaks, have fun."

Sally ended the call, took a sip from her cold coffee and shuddered. She went in search of a fresh cup and said hello to the rest of the team. "How are you all this morning?"

Everyone answered positively.

"Coffees all round?" she asked, feeling generous.

Lorne joined her at the drinks station and handed around the coffees. Sally stood alongside the whiteboard and picked up the marker. She noted down the very few facts they knew so far about the actual victim.

"As you can see up here, I've jotted down the name Bob Wallace. Has anyone heard of him?"

A sea of frowning faces stared back at her until Jordan clicked his thumb and forefinger together.

"The name rings a bell, but I'm having trouble working it out. Can we have a hint, boss?"

"He had a penchant for right limbs." Sally smirked.

Jordan tutted. "I know, wasn't he a serial killer who was caught a few years ago with a boxful of trophies?"

Sally winked at him. "You've nailed it. Now we've discovered another victim with the same MO as all the victims Wallace killed."

"Does that mean he killed this person, too?" Joanna asked.

"It's looking more and more likely, given the other

injuries the victim sustained. Lorne and I are going to visit the infamous Wallace this afternoon. Hopefully he'll be cooperative and confirm that the remains are those of one of his victims. The pathologist is aware of the situation, she's delving into things at her end; we're not sure where the other limbs are hiding at present. Once the pathologist locates them, she can do the necessary, matching any of the extra limbs to the skeleton, and bingo bongo, we've solved the case and we can add another life sentence to the one Wallace is already serving."

"If only life were that easy," Lorne mumbled.

Sally scratched her head. "Yeah, when I say it out loud it seems too good to be true, right?"

"I agree. Maybe we should be more cautious unless we want to end up with egg on our faces."

Sally nodded. "Party pooper. I know you're right, but maybe everything will slot into place without us breaking into our usual bucketload of sweat."

"What do you want us to do in the meantime?" Joanna asked.

"Keep digging. We still need to track down all the people who were reported missing between four and six years ago. I'm also waiting for our two inspector friends to get back to us about the previous farmer's children. Not that I'm holding out much hope that they'll be able to tell us anything. I'll chase them up later today if I don't hear anything by about four."

JUST AFTER LUNCH, at around two-fifteen, Sally received a call from DI Ramsey in Hereford. She took it in her office. "Hi, thanks so much for getting back to me so quickly. How did you get on?"

"Hi, to say the woman was a little cagey to begin with

would be an understatement. But the more she opened up, the more I believed she didn't know how the body got to be on the farm. She didn't work on the farm much, she lived there on and off over the years. Moved in with several boyfriends just to get away from the place. I asked her how long her mother had been dead, and she told me she'd died of breast cancer around fifteen years ago and her father never really recovered from her death."

"Could she tell you where her brothers live?" Sally asked.

"I'll send the address to you via email with my report. Sorry the news isn't better. I know how frustrating it must be for you to have a skeleton with no signs of evidence to begin your investigation. Maybe the brothers can offer you more. According to Lucinda, they worked on the farm now and again to help their father out when he was struggling to manage."

"At certain times of the year? When crops were growing et cetera?"

"I believe it was a cattle farm, not sure if he grew any crops or not. I didn't get the impression that she was hiding anything from me. She looked me in the eye throughout the interview."

"That's a good sign. I can't thank you enough for helping me out like this, thanks, Sara. If I can return the favour anytime, just give me a shout."

"Maybe I'll call in to see you if I ever decide to come over that way for a holiday on the Broads."

"If you've never visited the area, it is beautiful if you can get past how many murders happen around here."

They both laughed.

"Hey, likewise. I don't know about you, but our statistics have risen significantly since lockdown."

"You know what, I've never really considered that. My

team tend to work on the cold cases in the area, I guess that's why."

"Sounds like you have plenty of those around, otherwise you wouldn't have a specific team set up, would you?"

"It's a long story, one that involves a dodgy DI. Maybe I'll fill you in over a G and T one day. I've got to go now; we have a suspect we need to visit in prison."

"I don't envy you. Hope it goes well."

"So do I. Enjoy the rest of your day, and thanks again for going the extra mile for me."

"My pleasure. TTFN."

Sally shot out of her chair, fearing that time was slipping away from them. She hitched on her jacket and tore through the outer office. "Are you ready, Lorne?"

"I've been ready for the past ten minutes. We'll be pushing it to get there before three."

"It'll be a good excuse to use our blues and twos if we come across any heavy traffic. Keep up the good work, guys. We'll see you later."

Several "good lucks" followed them out of the door.

"Hang on, if I go any faster, I'll break my neck on these damn stairs," Lorne said.

"What's your problem? You're wearing flat shoes."

"My problem is I'm not getting any younger, and things that used to come naturally to me take longer to complete these days."

Sally laughed. "I must admit, never in my wildest dreams did I think I'd live to hear the great Lorne Warner use her age as an excuse at work."

"Sod off. That's not what I said at all."

Sally paused at the bottom and cocked an eyebrow. "Isn't it? Have you stopped your complaining now?"

Lorne growled and walked past her into the reception area.

"Off out, ladies? Have a good day," Pat said from behind his desk.

"It's quiet around here today, Pat. Not enough going on to keep you out of mischief, eh?"

"I have plenty of paperwork to keep me occupied, thanks, Inspector Parker."

"Haven't we all?"

They left the building, and Sally pressed the key fob to open the car. Once inside, she got on the road towards Norwich and brought Lorne up to date on what DI Ramsey had to say in Hereford.

"One down, two to go. It's not looking hopeful, is it?"

"Nope, not in the slightest. It was a long shot anyway, wasn't it? Now we've got Wallace in our sights. Did you get a chance to read the file, see where he disposed of his other victims?"

"The ones that were discovered weren't buried at all, they were mostly found in the open, in parks, woodland. One was located on the edge of a golf course, another in a supermarket car park."

"Interesting, I wonder why he decided to bury our victim."

"It's a question you need to ask him, not me." Lorne grinned.

"I'll make sure I do that. I'm slacking, I never got around to making any notes, I hate coming out here unprepared."

"Sorry, that's my fault for accepting the appointment without checking it was okay with you first."

"Don't be silly. You were forced to take the slot offered. I won't hold it against you. Can you do me a huge favour and jot some notes down for me while I drive?"

"Of course I can." Lorne removed her notebook from her pocket and poised her pen over a clean sheet. "Fire away."

They spent the next ten minutes going over what Sally should ask the prisoner.

"I feel much more prepared now, thanks, partner. How was Tony last night?"

"A bit stressed out. He was fine once we sat down and had a chat, though. What about Simon?"

"Pretty much the same. I bought him a special bottle of wine to add to his collection which cut through any grouchiness."

"Ah, there's method in your madness. I bet that cost you a penny or two."

"He's worth it. He's working extremely hard, they all are. He deserves a treat now and again."

They were nearing their destination. Sally could feel herself getting worked up. Coming here had always had an unsettling effect on her, what with Darryl, her ex, being imprisoned here. Life had been quiet lately in that respect. He'd carried out some despicable deeds in the past, mainly to make sure he was always in her thoughts after she'd put him inside for physically assaulting her several times.

Lorne sensed the change in her mood and nudged her. "Are you all right? Have your thoughts turned to Darryl?"

"You know me so well. I hate coming here in case I bump into him. I coped much better when they transferred him up to Scotland. It nearly killed me when they told me the prison up there was closing and he was being transferred back down here."

"That was a couple of years ago now. He hasn't been in touch since then, has he?"

"No, thankfully. But if he sees me walking down the corridors it might stir him into making a scene."

"I understand. The only advice I can give you is to try and suppress your emotions. You should feel safe in the knowledge that I'll be right there beside you."

"Lorne Warner, my heroine."

Lorne tutted and laughed. "Get away with you, all I was trying to say was…"

"You don't have to explain, I'm teasing. I am glad you're with me, though. Feel free to chip in during the interview. Your experience with the vilest of prisoners far outweighs mine."

"Don't worry, we're a team. You're never alone with me around, Sal."

Sally smiled and indicated to go through the prison gates. "Here we go."

"Chillax, we'll be fine."

Ken Pike, the new governor, was there to greet them once they'd passed through security. He shook their hands and introduced himself. "Nice to meet you both."

"We weren't expecting the red-carpet treatment, you meeting us like this, Mr Pike."

"I prefer to do things differently to my predecessors. I'm here to offer you all the assistance you need during your visit."

"My partner told me that you're expecting a visit from the top brass. Please, don't feel the need to babysit us."

"Far from it. I can tell you're both professionals. I'll leave you to it once we've passed through the next lot of gates, how's that? I just thought I'd come down here and introduce myself to you both."

"We appreciate it. How's the job going so far?"

"Pretty much as I expected. I'm hoping to make several changes in the coming weeks and months. I believe in treating the prisoners fairly. I refuse to lay down the law unless it is truly warranted. Most of the time that's not needed. The less hassle we have from the inmates the better life is for me and my officers, that's my aim at the end of the day. Treat people with kindness and understanding and they'll do the same to you."

"I hope it works out well for you, I really do. I'm aware there have been certain disruptive prisoners here in the past."

He leaned in and said, "Are you referring to your ex-husband, Inspector?"

Her cheeks heated up. "I am. You know about him?"

"I make it my business to know all there is to know about the prisoners. I'm also aware that he's caused you a lot of trouble on your previous visits. I want you to be assured that will never happen in the future, providing you give us prior knowledge of your arrival. He's locked in his cell and will remain there until you leave the premises."

A sudden gush of relief flowed through her veins. "That's great to hear, thank you for being so considerate."

"I aim to please. Here is where I leave you to it. Clive will take you to the interview room, and Wallace will be brought to you once you're settled. Any problems, don't hesitate to get in touch with me."

"You're too kind. Thanks for slotting us in at such short notice, and I hope the visit with the top brass goes well."

"I have every confidence it will, but thank you all the same. Good luck on your mission," he said with a smirk then turned right at the gates.

"He seems a nice man," Lorne said.

Clive was ahead of them and muttered, "He's introduced new measures that some of the staff are struggling to adjust to. It's early days yet."

"I'm sure his intentions are good," Sally replied.

"Let's just say the jury is still out for a lot of us. Here we are, ladies. You make yourselves comfortable, and I'll go and fetch the prisoner. I'm not sure what you feel about me remaining in the room during the interview."

"That would suit us, Clive. Thanks for the offer. What's Wallace like?"

He grinned. "You'll be able to make up your own minds about him soon enough. I'll be back within five minutes. Shall I organise some drinks for you? Cold would be better, that way the prisoner won't be tempted to do some damage with a hot drink."

"I hadn't thought about that. No, thanks, we're fine. We'll grab a coffee on our way back."

"As you wish." He opened the door and stood aside, allowing them to enter the cold, stark room that was no bigger than a cell itself.

Sally and Lorne rearranged the chairs and waited patiently for Wallace to arrive.

"How are you feeling?" Lorne asked.

"Okay, I think. Maybe a little anxious, but not as bad as I thought I would be. I think Pike's welcome reassured me."

"Glad to hear it. I think that's why he came down to see us. He seems a decent enough chap. I hope he accomplishes all he sets out to achieve. I'm undecided about his ethos, though, not for a prison."

"There are bound to be people who will stand in his way, you know what some folks are like about change. Whether they're a prison officer or a prisoner."

"I think he understands the task that lies ahead of him. I can hear footsteps."

Sally's stomach muscles clenched, and she clutched her hands together on the desk in front of her. "I'm ready for him."

"It's good to know Clive will be here on standby should we need him." Lorne removed her notebook and shoved it in front of Sally as the door opened.

Wallace's narrowed eyes were a warning sign to Sally.

"Hello, Mr Wallace. I'm DI Sally Parker, and this is DS Lorne Warner. Please take a seat."

He flung himself into the chair and glared at Sally. "I was watching *Judge Judy*, this better be good."

"We shouldn't keep you too long."

"Whatever, get on with it."

Wallace had a slight paunch, but other than that he seemed to be well toned. His chest was straining to be set free, and his shirt also seemed to be taut around his biceps. His brown hair was longer than his shirt collar, and his chin had a couple of days' growth sitting on it.

"I'm in charge of a cold case team, and this week we discovered the skeleton of a male in a field out near Acle."

"Good for you. What does that have to do with me?" He crossed his arms, putting an extra strain on his shirt in various sections.

"We're aware of the murders you committed and the fact that you chopped several limbs off your victims."

"Yeah, what about it? Every serial killer likes to leave their mark." He laughed.

Sally's stomach muscles clenched tighter. She inhaled a sneaky breath and discreetly released it. Lorne nudged her with her knee for added support.

"We're also aware that several unrelated limbs from your victims were also found at your house, and yet you've never admitted to killing more than the seven victims. Is the skeleton we uncovered another one of your victims?"

"You tell me. You cops seem to know everything, or think you do."

"We believe it is. Can you tell us the name of the victim?"

"Nope. They never introduced themselves to me. It's not like we ever went on any dates."

"So, all the people you killed were unknown to you, is that what you're telling us?"

"Read into my statement what you will. You ain't getting anything out of me, bitch."

"Wallace, watch that tongue of yours," Clive warned him from his position at the rear of the room.

Wallace turned in his seat and waggled his tongue at the officer. "What's it doing?" he asked and laughed. He was the only one who thought his joke was funny.

Clive ignored him and rolled his eyes to the ceiling.

"You guys need to tweak your sense of humour, it's lacking," Wallace said.

"How many more victims are there out there?"

Wallace shrugged. "I stopped counting."

"After how many?" Sally asked swiftly.

He pointed at her. "You'd have to get out of bed early to trip me up, Inspector, but keep trying. I'm finding our interview very amusing. I love seeing an SIO squirm."

"Is that why you toyed with DI Andrews four years ago?"

He wiggled his eyebrows and ran his tongue over his lips. "Made my day seeing that dickhead get all excited about ordering his men to dig a bunch of holes, only to find nothing. Being stuck in a cell all day, I had to get my kicks somehow."

Sally didn't rise to his taunts. "How many more victims of yours have yet to be discovered? And are the remains we found one of your victims?" she repeated.

"You tell me. You're the copper, not me." He smirked.

"Your house was located quite close to Acle," Lorne chipped in. "That makes you our number one suspect, especially if we take the condition of the remains into consideration."

"The condition?" He laughed again. "Oh, you mean the victim's right hand and right foot were lopped off? Any broken bones?"

"Yes, the tibia and fibula bones of both legs which was

also your signature, wasn't it? You might as well tell us the truth, the evidence is going against you anyway, and the CPS will have no trouble building another case against you, giving the family of your latest victim the justice they deserve."

He shrugged. "Sounds to me like you've got it all worked out for yourself, so why are you here, pestering me?"

"We're giving you the opportunity to tell us more about the victim. The more details you tell us at this stage the more it will go in your favour where the CPS are concerned."

"Are you crazy? I'm a lifer, it's not going to make a jot of difference to what the CPS are going to throw at me."

"Give us the name of the victim. Or at least tell us his story. How did you kill him?"

"Why should I make your life easier for you than it needs to be?"

"Do the right thing for his family."

"Spoken like a true professional who knows fuck all about the psychology of how a serial killer's mind works. Want to take me to the crime scene? I haven't jacked off for a while."

"Behave, Wallace," Clive warned for a second time.

"No, we won't be taking you anywhere. Clearly prison hasn't reformed you in the slightest."

"I didn't think it would. Are we done here? I find Judge Judy far more entertaining than a female inspector grasping at straws."

Sally cocked an eyebrow. "In your opinion. Reading between the lines, we've already obtained the necessary answers for us to bring our investigation to a close. You'll be hearing from the CPS soon, I guarantee it." Sally turned her attention to Clive and nodded. "We're done here."

Wallace tipped his head back and laughed raucously then slammed his hands on the table, making Sally and

Lorne jump. "Fucking coppers, you're all useless twats. I thought you'd be different. More fool me. I was willing to give you a chance, but I guess I was wrong. I see there's been no improvement since the judge decided to bang me up."

Clive marched towards them. "That's enough, Wallace. Back to your cell."

Wallace stood and glared at Sally. "Think you're good enough to take me on, bitch, think again. This isn't over, not by a long shot."

Sally held his gaze, her heart thumping wildly, rattling against her ribs. "It was nice to meet you, too. Have a nice life in your six-by-eight cell."

Clive intervened and pushed Wallace towards the door before he could fire off any further insults. The door slammed shut behind them, and Sally and Lorne let out a relieved sigh.

"Was that a threat?" Sally asked.

"It bloody sounded like one to me. Maybe that's all he's got left in his armoury these days. Ignore him. Let's get out of here. You promised me a coffee at a local hostelry, I seem to recall."

Sally smiled. "You win." However, she left the room with a gnawing feeling in her gut. She rubbed at her stomach.

Lorne inclined her head. "Everything all right?"

They started the walk back to the reception area.

"Let's just say my stomach has been put through the mill today."

"Maybe a brandy rather than a coffee should be on the horizon for you instead. I can take up the slack and drive back if necessary."

"That's a slippery slope I think we'd be foolish to go down. Come on, the sooner we get out of here the better."

"I agree."

The guard who'd welcomed them upon their arrival returned their personal belongings, and they set off.

"Hmm… we passed a pub on the way here, or was that my imagination?" Sally asked.

"Down the road on the right. So, a brandy is on the cards after all." Lorne grinned and slipped into the passenger seat.

"Hardly. Pubs usually sell a good range of coffees these days."

Sally parked close to the main entrance and ran in to check if the pub was still open, then she went back to the door and gestured for Lorne to join her. "What do you fancy? These are on me."

"A flat white if they have one, thanks. I'll grab a table."

Sally placed the order with the smiling blonde barmaid.

"I'll sort your drinks out and bring them over. Can I tempt you with a cream cake? We had a function on at lunchtime, and I think there are a few left over, free of charge, of course."

"How kind. I never say no to a cream cake. I'm sure my partner would love one as well."

"It's my pleasure. I won't be long."

Sally placed a tenner on the bar. "Is that enough?"

"It is. I'll bring your change over."

"No, keep it for a tip."

"You needn't do that, but thank you."

Sally joined Lorne at the table by the window. "What did you think of Wallace?"

"He's a tosspot. I can't even say he's the usual type for a serial killer because they're all different until you really scratch beneath the surface. To be honest with you, I thought he was going to sit there with his arms folded and go down the 'no comment' route. I suppose we need to count ourselves lucky he didn't."

The barmaid appeared carrying a tray laden with a plate

full of cream cakes and two cups and saucers. "Two flat whites and a little extra for your enjoyment, ladies."

"Wow, they look delicious," Lorne said, her eyes almost popping out of her head.

"I'll second that. Thanks very much." Sally smiled gratefully at the young woman.

"Enjoy. Give me a shout if you need anything else."

"We will. Is it always this quiet in here during the day?"

"We get the usual afternoon lull that generally allows me to do some cleaning and top up the bar. It's nice to see some new faces in here, though. Do you live in Norwich or are you visiting?"

"We're police, on a day trip to visit a prisoner."

"Ah, I had a feeling you were from the area. I hope your visit was fruitful?"

"It wasn't, but hey-ho. Thanks again," Sally said as if to dismiss the barmaid.

She took the hint and walked back to the bar.

Sally bit into one of the horns, and the cream oozed out of the side. She quickly wiped her mouth on a serviette. "Would it be cheeky of me to ask for a doggy bag? We could take the rest back to the team."

"Why not? You paid for them. Why did you get so many?"

"I didn't, they were free. Leftovers from a function they had earlier."

"Ah, I can understand your dilemma. Let's see how we get on first. If she sees us struggling, she might offer to box them up for us. Seems a shame to waste them, but I'm not about to sit here and eat two or three just for the sake of it. Getting back to our conversation, what was your take on Wallace?"

"Pretty much the same as yours. What's puzzling me is what he said at the end. I'm having trouble distinguishing if it was a threat or a promise."

Lorne shrugged and finished her mouthful before she

replied, "It might be a case of words are cheap and he just threw them out there to see the impact they evoked."

"Maybe you're right and it's not worth us worrying about." Something caught Sally's eye on the large TV screen in the corner. She slapped the table to get Lorne's attention and pointed.

The Breaking News headline read, *A skeleton has been discovered on a farmer's property in Acle.*

"Crap, that's all we need. How the hell did they get hold of the news so quickly?"

Lorne shook her head. "They have their ways, all dubious at the best of times. None of our team would open their mouths, so it would more than likely be from one of the techs at the lab. Perhaps they've got someone new working down there who hasn't had their induction or been informed about the protocol of dealing with the press after a find like this."

"Possibly. I'm still narked about it. We haven't had a chance to find the relatives of the victim yet. It's only going to put extra pressure on us. Sup up, we should get back to base, make that our priority now that the news has broken." Sally pushed her plate away, totally losing interest in the cream cake she'd only half eaten.

"Everything all right?" the barmaid called over.

"It was a lovely treat but far too much for us."

"I can sort out a box for you so you can take them with you."

"That would be great, thanks very much."

Lorne finished eating her cake, and the barmaid collected the plate and dashed into the kitchen. She returned with a cake box a few minutes later and placed it on the centre of the table.

"Here you go. The chef hates to see any kind of waste, so you really are doing us a favour."

"It's appreciated. We'll share them with our team when we get back to the station. If we're ever in the area again, we'll be sure to call in to see you. Maybe we'll have time to even sample your menu."

"You'll be very welcome. If you don't need anything else, I have to fetch some bottles from the cellar. I shouldn't be long."

"Feel free. We'll have our coffee and go."

The barmaid smiled and left them to it.

Five minutes later, Sally and Lorne were ready to go, but Sally refused to leave the bar empty while the barmaid was still absent. As soon as she returned, Sally and Lorne bid her farewell and left the pub.

Sally switched on the car radio to catch the news headlines on the hour, but the newsreader said nothing further than what had appeared on the TV screen back at the pub. She gripped the steering wheel until her knuckles turned white.

"Hey, I hope you're not getting yourself worked up into a state?" Lorne asked.

"No more than usual when someone has crossed the line. I always like to put myself in the shoes of the victims' families. All right, we have no idea who that is at the moment, but if anyone out there with a loved one or a relative on the missing persons' list sees that, can you imagine how distraught they could be right now?"

"I know what you mean. Let's not think too deeply about something that is out of our control."

"You're right, I'm sorry. I suppose Wallace got to me more than I was willing to admit. Effing cockwomble."

Lorne burst into laughter. "You crack me up, I haven't heard that name in years."

Sally sniggered. "I haven't either and I'm not sure where the heck it came from."

. . .

When they arrived back at the station, the other members of the team were unaware of what had appeared on the news. The atmosphere for the rest of their shift was gloomy, even the temptation of cream cakes failed to lift their mood. Just before the end of their working day, Joanna came up trumps. She called Sally over to her desk and told her the good news.

Sally sat next to her and asked, "What have you found?"

"As you know, I've been trawling through the missing persons' files for a potential match for the victim. I think I've discovered two distinct possibilities. Both males, same height as the skeleton at the mortuary."

"This is excellent news, Joanna, something for us to cling on to for a change. Can you bring up the two files for me?"

Joanna angled her computer screen towards Sally. "The first male is Connor Norton, although he lived a fair distance from where the remains were found."

"That doesn't matter, he might have been working in the area or visiting a member of his family, therefore, it would be foolish of us to rule him out. And the second one?"

"Is a Denis Short, he was a school caretaker in Acle but lived in Fishley, which is the next village. He went missing after a night out with friends."

"I've got a feeling he's the one, don't ask me how. Can you write down his address for me? Lorne, do you fancy taking a trip out to Acle? I know time is getting on, but I think it might be important."

Lorne shrugged. "It's fine by me."

"Ring Tony, and I'll prewarn Simon, tell him not to expect me home until later."

CHAPTER 4

Sally sucked in a breath and blew it out once she parked the car outside the small, terraced house in Fishley. "Are you ready for this?"

"I think so, are you?"

"I'll let you know afterwards. Let's go spoil the wife's evening."

"Hey, we don't know it's him yet. We shouldn't presume it is just because you have a feeling it is, Sal. Sorry, I'm not trying to tell you how to do your job, but…"

"You're right and I'm wrong. Our main aim should be to obtain the relevant DNA, if she has any lying around after all this time."

"Exactly. I know it's been a long day, but if you don't mind me offering you a bit of advice, I would tread carefully, for now at least."

"I will, I promise."

They left the car, and Sally rang the bell positioned in the centre of the front door. There was a lot of shouting going on inside the house. "Sounds ominous," she muttered. The door remained shut, so she rang a second time.

A man in his mid-to-late thirties opened the door. "What do you want? No, we don't need double glazing, but thanks for calling." He attempted to shut the door again.

Sally held up her warrant card. "Police. I'm DI Sally Parker, and this is my partner, DS Lorne Warner. Is Mrs Short in? We do have the right address, don't we?"

"You do. What do you want with her?" He looked Sally up and down and then did the same to Lorne.

"We'd like a brief chat with her, if it's convenient."

"Who is it, Lee?" A woman appeared behind him; she was a similar age. Her eyes were swollen and red.

Sally assumed she had been in tears moments earlier.

"Hello, Mrs Short. We're from the Norfolk Constabulary. Would it be convenient to have a chat with you?"

"Not right now, we're about to sit down and have our dinner," the man answered for her.

"Sorry to hear that. Maybe you can delay it five or ten minutes. I wouldn't normally ask, but it's important."

"Put mine in the oven, Lee. You're capable of dishing up your dinner yourself." Mrs Short didn't look him in the eye when she spoke.

"I shouldn't have to. I've been at work all day, the least you can do is…"

Mrs Short's eyes blazed. "Go on, say it. The least I can do is bow to your every whim once you step through the door in the evening. Screw you, pal. I'm an independent woman and I don't need you telling me what to do in my own home. Either you accept that or you fuck off and get a flat of your own again."

He grumbled something indecipherable and barged past her back into the house.

"I'm sorry. I didn't mean to treat him like that in front of you. He's pushed me too far tonight. We were having an argument before you rang the bell. He treats me like a slave most days, well, not today. I put my foot down, and he didn't like it. Tough shit. He can sod off for all I care. Bugger, I apologise, you don't want to hear about our rows. What can I do for you? Do you want to come in?"

"Thanks, it might be better," Sally replied.

She allowed them to enter the hallway and pointed to the first door on the right. "We'll go in the lounge; mardy arse will be eating in the kitchen. It's better to steer clear when he's in one of his moods."

Sally grinned and walked into the lounge, which was bigger than she anticipated, judging by the size of the house from outside. She and Lorne sat on the three-seater fabric sofa that had seen better days, and Mrs Short perched on the arm of an old leather chair.

"Now, what brings the police to my door?" she asked, a deep frown crinkling her forehead.

"I'm not sure if you've caught the news today or not, have you?"

"No. I was at work until three and I've been preparing the evening meal and doing the housework since I got home. You know what it's like, a woman's work is never done. Why should anything on the news concern me…? Oh God, unless… it's to do with Denis, is it?"

Sally held up a hand. "It might have something to do with your husband. All we can tell you right now is that the remains of a body were discovered yesterday. We've been through the missing persons' files and believe there's a possibility it could be your husband. We've narrowed the search down to two potential people."

Mrs Short slipped off the arm and into the chair. "I knew this day would come. I've never had the feeling that he was still out there, alive somewhere." She buried her head in her hands and cried.

Sally held back and gave the woman a moment. The door

to the lounge opened, and in walked the irate male they'd encountered earlier.

"Oi, what's going on here? What have you said to her?" He sat on the arm of the chair and flung a protective arm around Mrs Short's shoulders.

"They've found his body," she whispered.

"Who? What are you on about?"

Sally cleared her throat and filled the man in explaining that it *might* be Denis' body.

"Jesus, after all this time. Where? Did he jump in the river or something?"

"No, it was nothing like that," Sally said evasively.

"Well, what was it then? She has a right to know what happened to him. Why aren't you telling her?"

"I'm waiting until Mrs Short is ready to hear what I have to say."

"It's Frances," he shouted.

"Please, don't start, Lee. This has nothing to do with you," Frances said, her voice breaking.

"Fuck you. I know when I'm not wanted. I'll pack my bags and get out of your hair."

He stormed out of the room, and Sally was surprised that Frances didn't try to stop him. Instead, she shook her head, and fresh tears emerged and dripped onto her cheeks.

"Let him go. I don't give a shit. I'm at the end of my tether with him. He's a selfish bastard. He started off all loving; they all do until they worm their way into our homes, don't they?"

"I'm sorry he spoke to you that way. How long have you been together?"

"Three long years, emphasis on the long. Something snapped in me tonight, I don't usually fight back. I tend to take all the insults he fires at me without retaliating, but tonight was different. I've had my share of his bullying tactics to last me a lifetime. I'm better off on my own. God, this shouldn't be about me, not at this time. How will you be able to tell if it's Denis? Is his body... decomposed? I suppose it must be after all these years. I watch *Silent Witness,* so I know a bit about forensics."

"Do you have anything that belonged to Denis? Something that will allow us to compare a DNA sample? A comb perhaps, or his toothbrush? I know it's a long shot after all this time."

"No, I got rid of everything. I'm so sorry."

"It's no problem. In that case, we're going to need to match dental records. Can you remember what dentist he used?"

"Charters in Acle, we both went there."

"Can you give us your permission to obtain his files?"

"Of course. I can write a note for you now, or do you want me to give them a call in the morning?"

"If you could ring them tomorrow, that would be great."

Frances covered her eyes with her hand and sobbed. "After all these years, we can finally lay him to rest. If only you'd found him sooner."

Sally frowned. "May I ask why?"

"Both his parents died within six months of each other a couple of years ago. As soon as we registered him as missing, their health instantly deteriorated, as if they knew they were never going to see him again and they both gave up the will to live."

Unshed tears misted Sally's eyes. "I'm so sorry, that's terrible." She didn't really know what else to say.

"Lee's right about one thing," Frances said, "I have a right to know what happened to him, don't I?"

Sally cleared her throat and reached for Frances' hand. "Let's do all we can to identify him first and then we'll go over the details with you."

"It's bad, isn't it? I can tell by the way you're looking at me."

Sally tried to smile but didn't quite pull it off. "I'm not going to lie to you, it's not good."

A bang sounded overhead. "Tosser. When he gets a cob on him, everyone knows about it."

"Is he likely to kick off? Do you need us to intervene?"

"I don't think so. I've grown in confidence lately and I reckon I can handle him."

"We can hang around until he goes, just in case," Sally said.

"Would you? Thank you. It shouldn't take him long to pack his stuff, he hasn't got much."

Another thud sounded, and then heavy footsteps pounded on the stairs.

Frances sighed. "Here he comes. I won't be a moment; I think I should do this in private."

"Give us a shout if you need us. Good luck."

"Thanks," she mumbled and left the room.

Lee's voice was the only one they heard for a few seconds before the front door slammed.

Frances came back into the room and collapsed into her chair. She placed a front door key on the side table on her left. "He won't be coming back anytime soon."

"Will you lose any sleep over him?" Sally asked, her heart going out to the woman who had been hit by a double whammy in the last thirty minutes.

"No, I will not. He was an arsehole. I won't miss his misogynistic views that a woman's place should be in the kitchen, either. To be honest, I know you've come here to deliver the worst news possible, but I can't help feeling relieved that he won't be around to hamper the grief that I'm sure is going to hit me like an express train once you've left."

Sally removed a business card from her pocket. "Here's

my number, you can call me day or night. I want to assure you that I wouldn't dream of delivering this type of news and simply forget about you. Saying that, we still need to be cautious and make sure it is Denis' remains we've uncovered."

Frances placed a hand over her heart. "I can feel it in my soul. I've always known that he was never going to come back to me. My heart accepted it a long time ago—maybe that's why I moved on and welcomed Lee into my home—it's my head that will be the issue."

"Let's get the DNA sorted first and then go from there."

"I don't want you to think badly of me, but can I see him?"

Acid rose and burnt Sally's throat. She swallowed it down and said, "I really wouldn't advise it."

"Why? Don't you think it will give me closure? Isn't that usually why families visit their loved ones at a mortuary?"

"Only when there is a body to identify. In this case, there isn't. There are only remains, and I believe it will only upset you more if you saw them. But let's not jump the gun here, we'll get the DNA sorted first and then I'll leave you to have a word with the pathologist. I'm sure her advice will be the same as mine."

"So, what you're effectively telling me is that I should remember him the way he was and not sour the memories I have of him?"

"Indeed. I think it would be for the best, if the DNA results confirm the remains belong to Denis."

"This is so hard, knowing that you might have found him without being a hundred percent sure. His parents knew he was no longer with us, we all did. Sorry to keep repeating myself."

"Not at all. I must apologise for putting you in this position in the first place."

"I don't blame you, not in the slightest, you're only doing

your job. It must be so hard for you to visit people like me to share such life-changing news."

Sally shrugged. "It's part of our job, one that we have to get used to quickly. Are you sure you're going to be okay, in light of what has happened tonight?"

"I'll be better off now that he's left my home."

"Is there anything else we can do for you?"

"No. I could do with some time alone now, if you don't mind."

"Of course. You've got my number, don't be afraid to reach out."

Frances showed them to the front door. "I won't. I'll give the dentist a call in the morning to set the ball rolling. Will you let me know if it's him, as soon as you can?"

"Yes, you have my word." Sally shook Frances' hand and held it for longer than she would normally do. "Take care of yourself."

Frances smiled. "Don't worry about me, I'm pretty resilient when I want to be."

"And if you receive any backlash from Lee, let me know and we'll have a quiet word in his ear."

"I don't think he'll be back or cause any problems, but thank you, I'll be sure to ring you if he does. Enjoy the rest of your evening."

"You, too."

She closed the door gently behind them, and Sally heard the chain being attached which filled her with relief and a touch of confidence that Frances was going to be okay as far as Lee was concerned.

"Nice lady. Glad she ditched the boyfriend. I think we could both see through him when he pretended to care once he came back in the room. It didn't take much for him to kick off again," Lorne stated on the way back to the car.

Sally glanced around them before she opened the car

door and got in. "I wouldn't put it past him to cause her aggro, he seems the type."

"I'm sure she'll give you a call if he starts anything."

"I felt for her all the same. As if what we had to share with her wasn't enough to deal with for one evening, he decided to get in on the act as well. Selfish prick."

"I agree. She's well rid of him."

Sally started the car and dropped Lorne off outside her house fifteen minutes later.

"Don't let it spoil your evening. I'll see you in the morning. Usual time?"

"Yes, I have no intention of starting work early two days on the trot. Have a good one, say hi to Tony for me."

"I will. Try and put the case behind you and have a nice evening with Simon."

After Lorne left the car Sally continued her short drive home. Simon's Range Rover was parked in its usual place on the drive. She reversed and drew up alongside it and gasped when she saw the nasty dent along the entire left-hand side of the vehicle. "What the fuck? Why didn't he ring me?"

She collected her bag from the back seat and dashed into the house.

"Simon. Simon, are you all right?"

He was in the kitchen, stirring a pot on the hob. "I'm fine, why?"

"Why? Haven't you seen the state of your car? Don't tell me you hadn't noticed?"

He opened his arms, and she walked into them. They hugged each other tightly, and he kissed the top of her head.

"Everything is okay. Of course I knew about the damage. I'm not bothered about material things, you should know that by now."

With tears in her eyes, she glanced up at him. "God, I

thought you'd been in an accident and were hurt. You scared the crap out of me. What happened?"

"I'll fill you in over dinner. Are you ready?"

"Have I got time to get changed?"

"Five minutes."

Dex whimpered beside her. She sank down on her haunches to give him a hug. "What's the matter, boy, do you need a hug as well?" He rested his head on her shoulder, and she could tell he was shaking. "What's wrong with him? Oh shit, he wasn't sitting in the car when the accident happened, was he?"

"Go and get changed, we'll discuss it in a minute," Simon replied curtly.

Sally rose to her feet and tugged on Dex's collar, urging him to follow her, but he dug his heels in and refused to move. Something in his eyes worried her. She ran upstairs, quickly removed her clothes and slipped into her leisure suit. By the time she came back downstairs, Simon had dished up the spaghetti bolognaise and was opening a bottle of wine.

"Tuck in. I hope you're hungry. I made enough to put a couple of portions in the freezer as well."

Sally sat at the table and stared at him. Trying to work out why he was being so blasé about the incident that had clearly had a devastating effect on Dex. She'd only ever witnessed this level of fear in him once before, when Darryl had arranged for him to be dognapped.

Simon sat opposite her and passed her a glass of red wine. This evening, he didn't make his usual toast to their wealth and happiness.

Sally sat back and refused to pick up her fork. "Tell me what's going on, Simon."

"It was a slight knock. It happened at the auction house, correction, in the car park of the auction house."

"And? Was Dex hurt? Have you taken him to the vet?"

"Yes, what do you take me for? He was my main priority. The vet gave him a clean bill of health and told me I was worrying about nothing."

Sally peered under the table at her boy. "It doesn't look like nothing to me. He seems shit-scared. Has he been for a walk?"

"I took him for a long walk when we got home. Honestly, he's fine. Please don't make this out to be more than what it is, Sal."

She sat forward and frowned. "What? Both your car doors are buckled beyond repair, my dog is a shadow of his former self, telling me there's something seriously going on in that head of his, and you have the audacity to sit there and tell me it's nothing to be worried about? What the fuck is wrong with you? Do you know who did this?"

Simon's gaze dropped to his plate. He picked up his fork and stirred the sauce into the spaghetti.

"Simon? You do, don't you? Was the damage intentional?"

He took a sip from his glass and swallowed noisily.

"Jesus, say something. It's like getting blood out of a stone. What aren't you telling me? I have a right to know. You know how much I detest being kept in the dark."

"You're going to need to calm down, Sal."

"Am I?" Sally pushed her chair back and moved towards the worktop. With her back resting against the island, she folded her arms and demanded, "Either you tell me what's going on or I'll ring Tony to find out the truth, unless you've made a pact with each other, sworn yourselves to secrecy."

"Don't be so childish, of course we haven't. Sit down and I'll tell you."

"No. I'm all right where I am. Now tell me."

He glanced under the table. "You're upsetting the dog."

"Don't pull that one, he's the reason I'm so angry. Look at him, he's supposed to go to work with you and be safe.

Instead, I come home to find him trembling, shaken up. I demand to know why!"

Simon shoved his plate away from him and reached for his drink again. He paused to take a sip and then glanced up at her.

What she saw was pure fear in his eyes. She crossed the room and rested a hand on his shoulder. "You're scaring me, Simon. Please tell me the truth."

He ran a hand through his hair and chewed on his lip, worrying her even more. She squeezed his shoulder tighter.

"Tony and I were at the auction, bidding for a house that would be ideal to be converted into six flats."

He paused.

"And? Go on."

"And, we weren't the only party interested in it."

"Isn't that normally the case with conversions? What was different about this one?"

"It gathered a lot of interest, much more than normal, and from one party in particular."

"Who?"

Dex sensed the tension in the room and started to howl, which was unlike him.

She got down on her haunches again and called him. "Dex, hey, it's going to be okay, boy. Come here."

But he remained where he was, although he did cease his howling.

"God, between you, my anxiety levels are through the roof." She returned to her seat and took a sip of her wine. "I want the full story. Now."

"We outbid this guy, and the first thing he did was come over to us and tell us that we were going to regret buying the property."

"What? He threatened you? Did you tell the auctioneer?"

"Let me finish."

"Sorry. I'm listening. So what happened next?"

"Tony was the one who leapt from his seat and confronted him. He told the idiot to back off or there would be trouble."

"Shit. Good old Tony, ex-MI6 agent. Just what you didn't need."

"I know, but in fairness to Tony, he didn't know the guy was about to lose his rag."

"There, in the room?" Sally asked.

"No, he played it cool in the room. The bidding continued on three more properties. We both bid on a couple of the more interesting lots. He outbid me on one, and I did the same to him on the next one. Well, he was livid, absolutely seething. After the sale ended, he left the room. We thought everything would be fine and just put it down to experience. That was until we made our way out to the car and saw the damage to the Rover."

"He did that?"

Simon shrugged. "I can't tell you that for definite. It's a pretty big coincidence if he didn't."

"Fuck. Who was he? Do you know?"

"No. Tony and I didn't bother sticking around. My priority was getting Dex to the vet. Tony came with me. We took care of what was important to us. I couldn't give a damn about the car, that can be fixed."

"Thank you for putting our boy first, that means everything to me. But we can't let this goon get away with this. Taking revenge on people just for the sake of it when someone outbids him. He must have a bloody screw loose. Can you go back to the auction house tomorrow? They'll have a record of this guy if he's bought properties from them in the past."

"He bought a couple on the day. We'll do it tomorrow, if I can be bothered."

"What? You have to do it, Simon. He shouldn't be allowed to get away with this, it's not right. If you won't do something about it, then I will."

He sighed and rolled his head back to look at the ceiling. "I don't want to involve the police. It's my choice, Sally. We can get the car sorted."

Her temper flared. "So, you're going to allow him to get away with it, is that what you're telling me? Would you be saying that if he'd torched your car... with Dex inside?"

He stood and marched over to the sink and stared out of the window before he spoke again. He turned to face her. "Of course I wouldn't, stop putting words into my mouth. Whether you believe me or not, that dog means the world to me, too."

Sally walked towards him. "I'm sorry, I know he does. What I'm trying to do is make you see sense. If this guy has the front to cause that amount of damage to your car in broad daylight, what you should be asking yourself is what else is he capable of."

"I've thought about that non-stop since it happened, but if I involve the police then that's only going to make matters worse, isn't it?"

"Not necessarily and you need a crime number to claim on the insurance. We have to nip this type of thing in the bud before it gets out of hand. Wait a minute... You had a problem with someone vandalising a couple of your properties before they went to market a few months ago. Could that have been down to this guy as well?"

Simon shrugged. "I don't know, I suppose it's possible."

Sally stood there, her gaze flicking between her anxious dog still trembling under the table and her husband, who she could tell was truly concerned about what had happened, even if he didn't have the balls to come right out and tell her. It had been another long day, and her head was still full of the investigation, hampering her ability to think clearly. Suddenly, she experienced one of her light bulb moments and she reached for her mobile on the worktop.

"What are you doing? Please don't call the station, Sal."

"I'm not. Trust me."

She rang a number she used to call regularly and waited for the person to answer. "Hey, you, how's it diddling?"

"Hey, ex-partner, it's going okay. What about you?"

"I have a slight dilemma on my hands and wondered if you could pop over for a quick chat."

"What, now?"

"Only if it's convenient for you."

"Sure, I can be there in twenty minutes."

"Thanks, that'll give us a chance to have our dinner and clear up. See you soon, Jack." She ended the call. Simon was staring at her, his mouth hanging open.

"Jack? What can he do about it?"

"He's a PI, he has his uses."

"Bloody hell, how much is that going to cost us, or should I say, me?"

"Who cares? If he can solve the problem for us, it'll be worth it."

They returned to the table to complete their meals, even though neither of them was that hungry any more.

They managed to clear up the kitchen with two minutes to spare. Jack turned up on time and was pleased to see them both.

Sally hugged him. "Do you want a coffee or a beer?"

"I had a beer at home, I'd better stick to the coffee, thanks. What's going on, guys?"

"You two go in the lounge, I'll bring these through, we can speak in there."

"Is Dex all right?" Jack approached the table, and Dex cowered away from him. "Hey, it's me, boy."

"He'll be fine, leave him for now. He had a scare earlier and hasn't recovered from it yet. The vet has checked him over and can't see anything physically wrong with him. Mentally, on the other hand, well, that's a different story."

"Is that why you've contacted me?"

"Sort of. Go through with Simon, I won't be long. Can I tempt you with a chocolate biscuit? You missed out on some amazing cream cakes today, all free."

He grinned. "Just my luck. I never turn down food, you should know that by now."

"My memory isn't that bad, Jack."

He laughed and followed Simon through to the lounge.

Sally finished making the drinks and raided the cupboards for some chocolate biscuits. She put a selection on a plate and picked up the tray. "Dex, are you coming in with us?"

He sat there, staring at her, still trembling, although not quite so much.

"You're breaking my heart in two, boy. Come on. No one is going to hurt you here."

He stood and left the safety of the table but retreated as the anxiety mounted once he was out in the open.

She delivered the coffees and returned to the kitchen to try and coax Dex out with some of his favourite treats, but even they couldn't tempt him. "Stay there then until you feel safe." She bent down and kissed him on the head. He whimpered again, and she left the doors to the kitchen and the lounge open in case he changed his mind and decided to join them. "Have you told Jack?" she asked Simon.

"No, although he did notice the damage to my car and was asking what happened. I'll leave you to fill him in."

Sally spent the next five minutes doing just that.

"What the fuck? What a tosspot! Are you sure it was him who wrecked the Rover, Simon?"

"Pretty sure, but without the proof there's nothing I can do about it."

Jack took a sip from his mug. "And Dex was in the car when this guy attacked it?"

Sally nodded.

"Poor boy, no wonder he's out there crapping himself. Is there anything I can do to help? I'm guessing that's why you rang me."

"Correct. Simon didn't want to get the police involved as no one was injured, only the car was damaged, thank God, but it could have been a lot worse."

"Too right it could," Jack agreed. "This guy needs to be stopped. He can't go around attacking people's cars just because the auction didn't go in his favour. That's just sick. What do you want me to do?"

"Are you busy at the moment?"

"I've got a small job on the go. A woman who suspects her husband is having it away with his secretary, the usual mundane job, but I could run the two cases side by side, if that's all right with you? Sorry, I'm jumping in feet first as usual, if that's what you were asking. Was it?"

Sally laughed. "Glad to see your enthusiasm for your new role. Shame it dwindled while you were on my team."

"You know as well as I do that once we started working the cold cases my heart wasn't in it."

"I do. You told me often enough. What do you think, Simon?"

Her husband ran a hand around the back of his neck. It was a while before he asked, "What can we do about him?"

"I can gather the evidence and present it to him, warn him off, tell him that we'll get the police involved if he doesn't back off."

Simon scoffed. "I don't think he's the type to be warned

off by a harmless threat like that... not that I'm condoning anything else."

"In my experience, sometimes presenting them with the evidence and having a quiet word in their ear is usually enough to get them to rethink their attitude and actions."

"It's got to be worth a try, hasn't it? Simon has had problems with a couple of his properties being ransacked just before they were put on the market."

"And you think this guy might be behind that?"

Simon sighed. "I don't believe in coincidences, do you?"

"No, never. Can you give me anything about this guy? A name, what car he drives?"

"No, all I can do is tell you to go back to the auction house, see if they'll give you his details."

"That's not going to work, it's more than they dare do with the new GDPR laws in place. What about the properties he bought?"

"What about them?" Simon asked.

"I can do some surveillance outside one of the properties and wait for him to show up."

"Ah, yes, okay. Will it be all right to get Tony involved? He's got a better memory than me for all the nitty-gritty details you'll need."

"Go ahead."

Simon left the room to make the call.

Jack surprised Sally by taking her hand in his. "How are you holding up? The car's a mess, it must have come as a huge shock to you when you saw it."

Sally smiled even though she was hurting inside. "I'm okay. How are things at home now that you've left the Force?"

"They're okay, better than they were. The girls are behaving; no more grandkids on the horizon, so that's a huge relief. Oh, and Donna told me to send you her love and to tell you not to be a stranger."

"I'm thrilled for you, Jack, and is the business going well?"

"I'm surviving. Finding enough money to pay the bills and even managing to put some away for a holiday for Donna and me at the end of the season, you know, when it's cheaper and there are no screaming kids around the pools in Marbella."

"Hey, I'm so excited for you both." She peered over her shoulder and listened. Simon was still chatting to Tony. She leaned in and said, "And don't go giving us mates' rates, that's an order."

"What? I couldn't take the piss with you guys."

Sally raised an eyebrow and wagged a finger. "I'm warning you, he can afford it."

Jack shook his head. "We'll see. There's no way I'd rip my friends off, and that's final."

"I didn't tell you to double your rates for us, just don't give us a discount. What do you think's going on, off the record?"

"I'd say it sounds like another property developer has cottoned on to how successful Simon and Tony, and your father, of course, are in the business and is a tad jealous of their accomplishments."

"Seriously? What a frigging world we live in if that truly is the case. Successful people used to be applauded, and now, apparently, they're there to be bloody shot at and cut down to size."

"It's the nature of the beast. If this guy is being outsmarted by Simon and Tony at every auction, that's going to genuinely piss him off. It's bound to if he's self-employed and trying to make a killing for himself. Hasn't the property market changed recently? With the cost-of-living crisis and the mortgage rates going through the roof, not to mention the exorbitant costs of materials these days to actually carry out the renovations. If you take all of that into consideration, every property matters."

Sally was still considering his statement when Simon came back into the room.

"Tony and Lorne will be over shortly. What have I missed, anything?"

"Not really, we've just been catching up," Sally said. "Both of them are coming over? And they didn't mind?"

"No. Lorne is as upset about this as you are for some reason."

Sally turned away from her husband and rolled her eyes at Jack who suppressed a snigger by holding his mug up to cover his mouth.

They continued a general conversation until the others arrived.

"Hello, Dex, how are you?" Lorne asked in the kitchen.

Sally flew out of the lounge to greet them. "I'm glad you're here. Maybe you can work your magic on Dex. He hasn't come out of his hiding place all evening."

"I'm not surprised. When Tony told me what had happened, I was worried how the attack would have affected Dex. Give me a handful of treats, Sal, let's see if that will do the trick."

Sally crossed the room, and instead of bringing back a handful of treats, she brought the jar and handed it to Lorne. "I tried earlier, but it didn't make a difference. I'm more upset about how this has affected him than what happened to Simon's Rover, although that was bad enough."

Lorne stepped forward and gave Sally a hug. "He'll be fine. Dogs tend to live in the moment."

"You could have fooled me. He hasn't been right since the incident occurred. Simon got him checked over by the vet.

Physically he's all right, but as you can see for yourself, his mental state is questionable."

Lorne winked. "Leave him to me. You join the others, and Dex and I will sit out here having some quiet time together."

Tears pricked, and a lump formed in Sally's throat. "I just want my boy back. I hate to see him suffering like this."

Lorne held a hand up to Sally's cheek. "I know. Go. He's in the safest hands possible, I promise."

Reluctantly, Sally returned to the lounge, but not before she bent down and gave Dex an extra hug. She stood and wiped a tear that had slipped onto her cheek. She closed the door behind her so Lorne and Dex weren't distracted by the conversation going on in the lounge.

"Good news," Jack announced. "Tony can remember what properties this guy has bought over the last couple of months."

"I knew he wouldn't let us down. So when can you start, Jack?"

Simon was staring at the carpet, a pained expression contorting his features.

She kneeled in front of him. "What's wrong?"

He shook his head. "I'm scared—maybe not scared as such, but I'm very concerned that if we go after this moron, he might do something far worse next time. Shouldn't we be taking what happened to the car as a warning? Wasn't that what it was intended to be?"

Sally returned to her bean bag. "While I hear what you're saying, and on one hand you're right, but on the other, this dickhead can't be allowed to go around intimidating people like this, Simon. We have to nip this in the bud now before things escalate, surely you can see that? I'm right, aren't I, Jack and Tony?"

"She is," Tony agreed. "You need to listen to Sally. She's

never been one for revenge, that's not why we've brought Jack into the equation. Our main aim is to put a stop to this idiot's scare tactics before it goes too far and someone gets seriously hurt. My guess is that we're not the only ones he's pulled this stunt on. Look at it as we're doing what's right for the greater good and for other people's benefit as well as our own."

"Tony is right," Jack jumped in next. "You know me, Simon, I'm not one to just pile in there and stir up a hornet's nest with a large stick, but someone needs to have a chat with this fella, and soon."

Simon glanced up and held up his hands. "All right, stop bombarding me with reasons as to why we should do it. I'm on board with you and this chancy plan. What happens next?"

Everyone stopped talking when the door eased open and Dex wandered into the room with a smiling Lorne behind him.

"I think he was just after a little bit of sympathy, he seems to be right as rain now."

Dex approached Sally, licked her face and lay down beside her. "I can't thank you enough, Lorne. You've definitely got a knack with dogs and finding out what's wrong with them."

"I wouldn't say that. He's such a special dog. After what he went through today, he just needed to be reassured that he was safe."

"And he will be. I'm going to give Mum a call, see if she'll look after him during the day."

Simon started to object but thought better of it.

"It makes sense, love. Why should we take the risk? It will only be a temporary measure, until we sort out this thug."

Simon finally relented. "I can make a detour and drop him off at your mum's. If you think that's what is right for Dex?"

"I do."

"I think it's just what Dex will need," Lorne concurred, "and I know he'll get all the pampering he deserves from Sal's Mum."

"That's settled then. Dex's needs must come first."

"Have you managed to sort out the main problem yet?" Lorne asked, her question primarily aimed at her husband, who she squeezed next to on the sofa.

"I think we're all in agreement now. Jack is going to track down this guy from the information I'm going to give him, regarding a couple of properties I remember him buying, and we'll go from there."

Lorne faced Jack and warned, "My advice would be not to go in there heavy-handed."

Jack nodded in agreement. "I won't. I'll see how the land lies with him first, follow him discreetly for a few days, if only to get a rough idea about how he operates. If I see him causing problems at any other developers' sites in the area, then I'll have no reservations about calling for reinforcements. Umm... that'll be you and Sally."

"We'll be up for that, won't we, Sal?"

Sally sniggered and rolled her eyes. "I suppose. It's not like we have anything else on our plate at the moment." She stood and topped up their drinks.

Jack was the first to leave with a promise that he would do his best to get back to them within a few days with any information he'd gathered.

Sally showed him to the front door and hugged him. "Thanks for doing this for us, Jack, it's truly appreciated."

"I know. I hope I don't let you down."

"Never... umm... well, let's not go that far, going on your past performance on the Cold Case Team."

"Yeah, the less we say about that the better."

She kissed him on the cheek and closed the door behind

him then returned to the lounge to find Dex had moved and was now sitting next to Lorne, having a cuddle.

Another ten minutes, and Tony and Lorne announced they were leaving as well.

Finally alone, Sally sat next to Simon with Dex glued to her leg. "That turned out to be a good evening, after all."

Simon put a finger under her chin and forced her to look him in the eye. "I love you, Sally Parker, more and more each day. I don't know how I would have coped with all of this if I didn't have you by my side to steer me in the right direction."

"Nonsense. We're all in agreement, this guy needs to be stopped, and we're the team to do it, compared to a bunch of novices taking him on. I doubt if you're the only one he's tried these awful tactics with, Simon, but between us, we can make sure it's the last time he bullies a competitor."

He kissed the top of her head. "I hope you're right. I could do with an early night, how about you?"

She glanced at the clock on the wall; it was already ten-thirty. "Blimey, where has the evening gone? Come on, boy, time to put you in the garden."

"I'd rather go to bed." Simon laughed.

Sally tutted. "Lucky we haven't got a doghouse in the garden. If you hadn't agreed to our proposal this evening, you might have found yourself sleeping out there instead, for the foreseeable future."

"Charming."

She kissed him and grinned.

CHAPTER 5

The next few days were riddled with frustration for Sally. The team had done their very best to try to locate the family of the other missing person, who the remains might belong to, but each avenue they went down they drew a blank. Now it was a waiting game to see if the dental records they had obtained and passed on to Pauline were a match for Denis Short.

Eventually, that confirmation came through from the lab, and Sally and Lorne had returned to Frances' home to deliver the news. Frances had sat there stunned for several minutes, just staring at the wall, until Sally had asked if she was okay. Frances then admitted that the news had given her the closure she had required to get on with her life without the need to feel guilty. She also told them that thankfully, Lee had neither returned to the property nor contacted her since he'd walked out of the house on Sally's last visit.

With the identification now to hand, and the file regarding Bob Wallace's involvement in Short's death on its way to the Crown Prosecution Service, it was time for them to type up their reports and put the investigation to bed. At least, that was the intention, until Joanna received an alert on the system that put that particular theory in jeopardy.

"Boss, I think you should see this."

Sally shot across the room and read the screen over the sergeant's shoulder. "What the...? I can't believe what I'm reading."

"What's wrong?" Lorne asked. She joined them and read the information on Joanna's screen for herself. "Holy shit, this can't be right, can it?"

"Who is the SIO on the case, Joanna?" Sally asked, her mind whirling up a storm of confusion.

"DI Helen Edmonds."

"Thanks, I'll contact her." Sally went through to her office to make the call, hoping the journey would help clear her mind and make some sense of what might be going on. It didn't. She rang Edmonds who was in the Murder Investigation Team. "Hi, this is DI Sally Parker of the Cold Case Team. Do you have time for a brief chat, Helen?"

"Sure. There's a bit of a lull around here at the moment. You know what it's like when you're waiting for all and sundry to get back to you, especially the lab with vital information. Do you want me to pop up and see you?"

"Perfect. See you soon." Sally reached for the file on her desk that she was hoping to transfer to the archives later that day and rejoined the rest of the team. "She's on her way to see us now."

"Reading through the notes, the victim was found a few days ago. I can't help wondering why Pauline hasn't contacted us," Lorne said, her brow furrowed into deep creases.

Sally sighed and nodded. "I was wondering the same thing. Don't worry, I'll be having words with her after I've got all the facts from Helen. Anything like this should have been brought to my attention immediately. If Joanna hadn't set up an alert, we'd be none the wiser now."

The conversation went back and forth between them for the next ten minutes until Helen Edmonds entered the room, then everyone fell quiet.

Sally shook her hand and welcomed her. She introduced the members of her team to Edmonds and offered to make her a coffee.

"Thanks, I can't remember the last time I had one, which is unusual for me. How can I help? You were a little reluctant to tell me over the phone, at least, that's the impression I had."

Lorne insisted on making the coffee while Sally went over the investigation they believed they had just put to bed.

Helen perched on the desk behind her. "What? None of this is making any sense. You think there's a connection?"

Sally crossed her arms and tapped her foot without even realising it. "Don't you? Your victim was found with broken lower legs, his right foot and right hand removed, the same as Denis Short plus the other victims Bob Wallace is behind bars for."

"Jesus, this can't be right. But the case I'm dealing with isn't a cold case. The victim was murdered in the garage he runs. Two mechanics showed up for work the next morning and found their boss lying in the inspection pit, under the car he'd been working on.

"I need to speak with Pauline, see what she thinks. However, the last thing I want to do is step on your toes, Helen."

Edmonds shrugged. "It makes no odds to me. I'm as perplexed about this as you are."

Sally reached for the nearest phone and rang Pauline's direct line at the mortuary. Fortunately, she caught her at the perfect moment, sitting at her desk, preparing paperwork for the post-mortem she had performed on the victim in question.

"Hello, Sally, what can I do for you?"

"Hi, Pauline, how do I say this…? Let's try it this way: have you got something to tell me?"

There was a pause on the other end of the line. "Er… can't think of anything, no."

Sally's foot tapped faster. "Let me jog your memory… What about the victim you've recently conducted a PM on for DI Helen Edmonds?"

Another pause followed, and then Sally picked up that Pauline had swallowed and muttered the word *shit* under her breath.

"And?" Sally pressed, her adrenaline pumping.

"And, bugger, I should have made the connection earlier and… I didn't. Now I'm sitting here kicking myself in the shins."

"We're coming over to see you. Now."

"Okay, I'm sorry, Sally. You're right, I should have made the connection sooner and got in touch with you."

"No shit, Sherlock." Sally slammed the phone down and paced the room. "Un-frigging-believable. What the fuck is wrong with her? Has she done this on purpose?"

"I doubt it," Lorne said. "You're going to need to calm down before you face her, Sal."

"Seething isn't the bloody word. That woman is seriously ticking me off. I know she's new to our patch and she has massive shoes to fill, which is probably a huge pain in the rear for her, but Jesus, she needs to do the right thing and get her head down and give her all to every investigation."

Helen raised a hand. "In her defence, I've worked with her a few times over the past year or so and she's always come across as an utter professional. Shoes to fill? What am I missing?"

Lorne was the first to speak. "Sally is married to Simon Bracknall, the former pathologist for the area."

"Ah, right, I get it now. Forgive me for not making the connection earlier. I take it you're still using your former name just because it's easier?"

Sally nodded. "Yep, I couldn't be bothered to take on the hassle involved in changing my name while still on the Force."

"I see. Don't shoot me down in flames here, but would that be why you're coming down heavily on her?" Helen suggested.

"Not at all. I expect professionalism at all times from those around me. If they're not prepared to give it their all, one hundred percent of the time, then they shouldn't be in the damn job."

Helen sighed. "I agree. Hey, maybe we should give her the benefit of the doubt, what with your investigation having to do with a cold case."

"Nope, I can't get over the fact that she didn't pick up on the same MOs in both cases. It couldn't have been clearer."

"All right," Lorne interjected, "I think we'd better leave it there for now. I can't see how going round and round in circles is going to help."

Sally shrugged. "You're right. We should get over to the lab. Are you going to come with us, Helen?"

"I wouldn't miss it for the world. Ouch, that sounded like I'm looking forward to you giving Pauline a pasting when we get there, but that's not what I meant at all. What I was trying to say is that I'm aware of your reputation, or should I say reputations, and I'd consider it a genuine honour to be involved in an investigation with you both."

Sally cringed at the prospect of Helen gushing around her, more than likely hanging off Sally's every word. "Let me get one thing straight from the outset: this is your investigation, we're simply tagging along for the ride due to the links to our investigation, a crime that took place around five years ago."

"Yes, yes, of course. I wholeheartedly agree with you. However, if you believe I'm going about the investigation the wrong way, please, don't hesitate to jump in and pull me up on it."

"Don't worry, I won't. Just conduct your enquiries as you would usually go about them."

"I'll do that. Thank you. I just need to go back to the office to collect my phone and handbag. Shall I meet you outside in ten minutes? I'm based at the other end of the station."

"There's no rush, take your time."

Helen left the office.

Sally sat in the chair beside her and put her head in her hands. "What are we letting ourselves in for here?"

Lorne stood next to her and chuckled. "Ah, the enthusiasm of a young cop, eager to please her 'infamous superiors', and yes, I'm joking. Hey, don't tell me you weren't tripping over yourself doing all you could to impress your colleagues who had been on the Force for decades?"

"Er, not to my knowledge. I took every day as it came and treated those with experience around me with respect. I've never knowingly licked anyone's arse in my rise up the ladder. Be honest, have you?"

Lorne cocked an eyebrow. "I think you know the answer to that as well as I do."

Sally shuddered. "I hope she's not going to become a pain in the arse. I have enough on my plate as it is, dealing with the temperamental Pauline. She needs to get her act together and swiftly, otherwise, if things like this continuously crop up, she's going to find, in no time at all, she loses the respect of the professionals surrounding her."

"You said it yourself, she's still finding her feet in the job.

Maybe she hasn't had a lot of time off lately. Perhaps she's been going from one case to the other without switching off in between."

"Stop making excuses for her. She was in the wrong on this one, even you have to admit that, Lorne."

"She was, I agree, but now is not the time to come down heavily on her."

"Why?"

"Because there's a possibility she might take umbrage and stop being so obliging with us."

Sally frowned. "How is she ever obliging with us?"

"The PPE aspect, she's always giving us supplies when she doesn't have to."

"All right. Fair point. Okay, let's get ready to rumble, and I promise to hold my temper in check when we get to the mortuary."

"Excellent, I'm sure it'll work in your favour in the long run. It's never a good idea falling out with a pathologist."

Sally didn't respond, but she knew Lorne was right. There was no point in falling out over what might turn out to be a genuine mistake, because it could indeed sour a relationship with Pauline that she might regret one day.

THEY TRAVELLED SEPARATELY in two cars until they reached the mortuary. Helen followed Sally and Lorne and remained a few steps behind them as they walked through the corridors to Pauline's office. However, the pathologist was nowhere to be seen.

"Jesus Christ, I told her to expect us. Where the hell is she?" Sally complained after finding her office empty.

"I'm here. Sorry, a girl has to pee now and again," Pauline hollered from the other end of the corridor.

I take it back. I must give her a chance; I don't want another lecture from Lorne on the way back to the station. Sally glanced at Lorne and smiled.

She could tell Lorne was suppressing a giggle, and her eyes held a warning for her to behave and not to rock the boat.

"Hi, shall we make ourselves comfortable in your office?" Sally asked.

"Yes, I'll fetch a couple of extra chairs from the room next door," Pauline called back.

"I can do it," Helen offered enthusiastically. "Which office, left or right?"

"Your right," Pauline shouted.

Sally and Lorne entered the office. Sally insisted Lorne should take the seat already there and waited for Helen to bring the others in. As it was, Pauline lent her a hand.

Pauline's cheeks had a higher colour to them than normal, and she avoided eye contact with Sally, which amused her.

They all took their seats, and it was Pauline who plucked up the courage to speak first.

"Again, I must apologise for my mistake. In my defence, I have been snowed under this week with ten PMs and, as you can imagine, with all the paperwork involved for each examination, I haven't had time to think what day it is, let alone whether your two cases might be connected." Pauline still didn't cast a glance in Sally's direction. If anything, her apology was directed at Helen.

Sally struggled to bite her tongue. "Apology accepted. I just hope there's nothing more to do with this than meets the eye."

Pauline shot her a worried glance. "What are you saying? That it was intentional on my part?"

"Cards on the table… Since you've arrived, I've sensed

some tetchiness between us, which appears to have got worse in the past few weeks."

"I... I... no, that's clearly not the case at all. Again, the most I can do is apologise if my behaviour towards you has been questionable at times."

"Why? Can you explain why you've got a problem with me? Is this more to do with my husband?"

"Absolutely not." Pauline's voice rose several octaves. "Honestly, I don't know why my behaviour is different when I deal with you as opposed to the other officers in the Norfolk Constabulary."

Sally inclined her head and knocked her knee against Lorne's. "So, you're openly admitting that there is a problem between us?"

Pauline interlocked her fingers. "This isn't the direction I expected this conversation to take. All I can do is apologise again for anything I have ever said out of turn."

"Give her a break, Sally, she's apologised enough now," Lorne said.

"Okay, can I suggest we call a truce and, going forward, promise that we will treat each other with the respect we both deserve?"

"I agree. Feel free to pull me up if I slip up again in the future."

Sally shook her head. "I shouldn't need to do that, not now you've given me your word that your attitude will change from this day forward."

"Now, can we get down to the real reason we're here?" Lorne asked.

"Did you find any evidence at the scene that could lead us back to Bob Wallace, the killer of Denis Short, our cold case victim?" Sally asked.

Lorne removed her notebook, and Helen followed suit.

"I can't answer that specifically because, I reiterate, I

hadn't made the connection between the two cases until you rang me. I must admit that evidence has been very thin on the ground. All we've gathered so far is a muddy footprint found at the entrance of the garage."

Helen looked up from the notes she was taking. "I wasn't aware of that."

"It only came to my attention this morning. Again, I must apologise for not letting you know, DI Edmonds. It was very remiss of me."

"Can I just make an observation?" Sally asked.

"Please do," Pauline replied and winced as if sensing she was in for another reprimand.

"If you're as snowed under as you say you are, why haven't you asked for support?"

"The department is short-staffed. It's something we have to accept and get on with."

"Have you got an assistant lined up yet?"

"One is supposed to be coming my way in the next month or so. In the meantime, it's up to me to pick up the slack. Most of the time I can cope, but when the pressure builds like it has this week, I dare even the most resilient of professionals not to struggle."

"Are you getting enough sleep?" Sally asked, suddenly feeling guilty for tearing a strip out of the pathologist, who was obviously under the cosh.

"The past week I have slept in the office and managed to grab anything between two and three hours sleep per night."

"Not good enough. That's when mistakes are bound to happen, as we've proven today."

Pauline held her palms upwards and shrugged. "You tell me what the solution is, because every other pathologist I have held a conversation with lately has told me they're in the same boat. Mistakes are bound to happen, aren't they?"

COULD IT BE HIM?

Sally cleared her throat and fidgeted in her seat. "I feel for you. Sorry for coming down so heavily on you earlier."

Pauline smiled. "You had a right. I should have been more alert. Let's put all this behind us and move on, decide what we need to do to put the situation right."

"If there's no evidence pointing towards Wallace being involved, surely that can mean only one thing," Lorne stated.

Sally turned her way and gasped. "Don't tell me you're suggesting we've got a copycat killer on our hands?"

Lorne faced her. "What else could it mean?"

"Helen, as SIO, will you give us permission to read the PM report of your victim?"

Helen's nod was enthusiastic. "Gosh, yes, please do."

Pauline hurriedly searched the files in her trays until she found the one relating to Andrew Grant and handed it to Sally. She opened the folder and placed it between her and Lorne so they could flick through it at the same time. "Give me a thumbs-up when you've read it and I'll turn the page."

Lorne gave her the thumbs-up in response.

The room fell silent, except for the odd rustle of pages here and there until Sally and Lorne had speed-read the file.

Sally passed it back to Pauline. "We've got the gist of it. Any idea what type of weapon the killer used?"

Pauline inhaled a breath. "If I were to hazard a guess at this stage, I would say it was either a very large knife, a machete, or even an axe."

"There were wounds to the man's stomach and chest. Denis Short also had wounds to his stomach, judging by the nicks you found in his rib cage. So that's yet another similarity between the two cases, not that we needed one."

"And yet another point I missed," Pauline whispered, her head dipping.

"Stop it. It wasn't a dig, I was merely stating facts," Sally admonished her. "With so many wounds, I'm assuming it will be impossible to tell us what the cause of death was?"

"I said pretty much the same thing in my report. Several major organs were struck, judging by the blood found at the scene and what I discovered during the PM. In my personal opinion, he bled out. Whether that was the killer's intention, we won't know until they've been caught."

"Do you have any leads at all on the case yet, Helen?" Sally turned to the younger detective and asked.

"Nothing substantial, not yet. When I visited the wife with a colleague of mine—my full-time partner is on maternity leave at present—she wasn't really up to speaking much, so I left. Grief is such a personal thing. In my limited experience as an Inspector so far, people react very differently when they've been told their loved ones have passed. Mrs Grant instantly melted down and demanded to be left alone. I tried to call her first thing this morning and, again, she told me she was too upset to speak with me. I'm not sure what I can do to get around that."

"Sometimes the need to be compassionate but forceful has to come into play. If you'll allow us to, we'd be willing to give it a try. During the initial stages of an investigation, it's always advisable to question the closest relatives to ask if there have been any incidents in the victim's past that could have led to their murder."

"Feel free. I think we should run this as a joint investigation now, if you're up for that? I'm sure my DCI would jump at the chance to have me working with two well-respected officers such as yourselves."

Sally faced Lorne to get her approval. Lorne winked at her, and that was enough for Sally to accept.

"We'll need to run it past our respective DCIs, but I really don't think there will be an issue, not if there are links to both cases. It would be in all of our interests to arrest the killer. Without a confession from Bob Wallace about the Denis Short murder, there's every chance that he could have been killed by someone else. That someone being the same person who killed Andy Grant."

"That's a hell of a coincidence," Lorne suggested.

"I know but I don't think it's something we can rule out. I bet the CPS come back and question the lack of evidence connecting Wallace to the cold case murder."

"You think that's possible?" Lorne asked.

Sally chewed her lip and shrugged. "The more I think about it, the more likely I believe how probable it is. If the latest victim hadn't turned up, let's face it, we would have considered it a slam dunk that Wallace was the culprit. Grant's death has definitely got us thinking, hasn't it?"

"I think Sally is right," Pauline admitted. "Just because everything is pointing at Wallace right now, without the evidence to back it up, we're up shit creek."

"Then the technicians need to come up with something substantial from both crime scenes," Helen said.

"That's going to be tough with our victim, who was murdered around five years ago," Sally muttered, her thoughts running away with her.

Lorne nudged her. "I know that look. What are you thinking?"

"Going back to the copycat aspect, what if Denis Short was killed by a copycat killer five years ago and the person went to ground after he committed the murder?"

"A killer with a conscience? Is that what you're saying?" Lorne asked.

"Possibly. Maybe the murder took too much out of them. He or she would have needed to have dug the grave out at the farm on the night of the murder. That in itself must have been exhausting, let alone carrying out the injuries sustained by the victim."

The four of them mulled over Sally's theory, and then Helen jumped in and said, "What if the killer then saw the news coverage this week and decided to put us off the scent by killing someone else, namely Andy Grant?"

Sally shrugged. "It's plausible. Without a confession from Wallace in prison and crucial evidence to place him at the scene of both murders, we're stumped, or we weren't, until Andy Grant's body showed up."

"As much as I hate to admit it, I think you're right, Sally. Maybe the copycat killer struck before and has suddenly resurfaced to give this killing lark another go. Their aim, to go down in history as yet another warped serial killer."

"Until we have firm facts and evidence at our disposal then anything is possible," Sally replied reluctantly.

"I'll get on to the lab, impress upon them the importance to give each crime scene a thorough search, not that they don't usually, but it won't do any harm to point out the obvious to them," Pauline said. She picked up the phone and issued her instructions.

While Pauline was on the phone, Sally leaned forward and whispered to Lorne and Helen, "Our first step is to get the authority we need from our DCIs to work together. There's no point in going any further with this at the moment until we have that in place. Are you all right with that, Helen? Who is your DCI?"

"Anne Cummings. I have every confidence she will agree to it. What about yours?"

"Mick Green. He might take some persuading, but I've managed to do that successfully a few times over the years. I'm sure he'll give us the go-ahead."

"He'd be foolish not to," Lorne agreed.

Pauline ended her call. "They're going to do their very best for us, although the garage, the second crime scene, is open again. I'm sorry, ladies, time is marching on, and I have a heavier schedule than usual ahead of me in theatre today."

"We'll let you get back to it, Pauline," Sally replied. "Thanks for sparing us the time to go over all of this today."

"It was worth it, even if all it has done is clear the air between us."

"I agree." Sally smiled and rose from her seat. "Good luck. Keep us informed when you get a spare moment."

"Don't worry, I've learnt my lesson on that one. Speak soon."

The four of them left the office, and Pauline headed off in the other direction, while Sally, Lorne and Helen walked up the corridor to the car park.

"If we give our DCIs a call now then we can get on with the investigation without any further delay. Helen, don't take no for an answer. Be prepared to speak up for yourself if necessary. We all know it makes sense for us to work alongside each other, we just need to convince Cummings and Green it's the right thing for us and for the victims' families."

"Leave it with me. I'll keep my eyes shut and fingers crossed throughout the conversation. That has paid off for me in the past."

Sally's eyes widened. "Seriously?"

"No, I was winding you up. Cummings is a pussycat."

"We'll leave you to it then."

They sat in their cars and placed the calls. During her somewhat strained conversation with DCI Green, Sally took a sideways peek at how Helen was getting on. Instead of looking anxious, Helen was smiling and nodding during her exchange with Cummings.

Lorne jabbed Sally in the thigh and punched the air with her fist, in other words, urging her to give DCI Green what for.

"I'm sorry, sir, I think you're wrong. It makes sense to join forces to see where it leads us. The minute I think the investigation is slipping away from us, you have my word that I will back off and leave DI Edmonds to get on with it."

"Your word, eh?" Green countered. "Okay, you have a limited time on this, DI Parker. No more than a week, you hear me?"

"I do, sir. I have every confidence in my team that we'll be able to wrap things up in that time." She faced Lorne and grimaced, then mouthed, "What am I saying?"

Lorne placed a hand over her mouth to suppress a giggle.

Sally ended the call, exhaled a large breath and rested her head against the headrest. "Holy shit! I didn't expect it to be me who would be under the microscope."

Lorne leaned forward and peered into the other car, and Helen was smiling, borderline laughing, while she was still talking on the phone.

"Yeah, I think Helen's wariness was misplaced by the look of things."

"Bully for her. Green can be such a wanker at times."

"Hey, he's a kitten compared to Sean Roberts, my former DCI. I think Katy and Charlie will vouch for me on that one. According to Charlie, he's always coming down heavily on Katy when she least expects it."

"Arsehole. Men like that make me sick. I suppose we're talking about the Met here. Enough said, eh?"

"Yeah. I'm glad to be out of it. It was bad enough in my day, let alone what's going on nowadays, if the news reports are to be believed."

"The less said about that the better. Come on, Helen. Has she given you the go-ahead or not?"

Seconds later, a beaming Helen jumped in the back of Sally's car. "Umm... well, I wasn't expecting her to be so obliging. She turned out to be putty in my hands."

"Wow! Great result." Sally resisted the urge to reply through gritted teeth.

"It was a no-brainer once I mentioned who I would be working with," Helen gushed.

"Okay. So, where do we go from here? I think our first stop should be to look over the crime scene at the garage to get a feel for what went on there. Are you agreeable to that, Helen?"

"Sure. Wherever you want to begin is fine by me, Sally. Do you want to follow me?"

"Why not? Let's get this show on the road and see if, between us, we can try and figure out what we're up against here."

CHAPTER 6

When they arrived, they found the garage open for business. Inside, were the two brothers who'd discovered their boss the morning following his murder. But Sally felt the men seemed a little subdued.

She and Lorne produced their warrant cards.

"We promise not to get in your way," Sally said.

"Sure, we'll leave you to it. DI Edmonds can run through where… it happened. We've got paperwork to sort out and customers to ring," Sean said.

"Thanks. We might follow up with some questions later, if that's okay with you?"

"It's fine," Chris Watts said.

The two men walked away and entered the office.

Helen led Sally and Lorne over to the murder scene. "It happened around here. You can still see remnants of the patch of blood we found. Pauline suspected Grant's body was rolled into the inspection pit after he was murdered."

"Do you know what time he was killed?"

"We believe he was here alone, working on a car that had a problem with it that the boys had failed to pick up on during the day. Grant insisted that he would complete the job and told the boys to leave at about six-thirty. Apparently, they closed the door behind them but left it unlocked."

"So, the killer had access without needing to alert Grant." Sally peered over her shoulder at the door. "Was the music on?"

"The boys said their boss refused to work without it."

"That would explain how the killer managed to surprise the victim, if that's what happened. Maybe they gained access and hid until Grant came out of the pit, perhaps to fetch more tools for the job in hand."

"That was my assumption as well," Helen agreed. "The killer then carried out the deed and left via the door which was unlocked when the fellas got here at eight the following morning."

Sally and Lorne walked the area.

"Was one of the injuries a bang to the head?" Sally asked.

"Yes, but Pauline admitted it wasn't hard enough to kill him."

Sally lowered her voice and asked, "What did the brothers have to say?"

"In what respect?" Helen replied, confused.

"I'm presuming you asked them about any likely suspects?"

"Ah, sorry. Yes, I did. I interviewed them separately, and they both told me the same. That Andy was a likeable man, never had any issues with customers paying for the work they'd had done."

"Did you ask them if they've seen anyone hanging around lately? Or if Andy had mentioned if he'd fallen out with a neighbour or something along those lines?"

"I did. I asked all the usual questions, and neither of them said anything untoward had happened to Andy, not that they were aware of."

"Okay, what about the owner of the vehicle he was working on?"

"Nope, the same. He collected the car the following day, or at least tried to. I was here when he showed up. He was upset by the news and agreed to come back to collect the car. The twins said he was a decent chap, had been bringing his car here for years to be serviced and if anything went wrong with it in between."

Sally ran a hand around her face. "It's perplexing that the techs didn't find any evidence here."

"An ultra-clean crime scene usually means only one thing," Lorne said.

"I agree, that the crime was premeditated and the killer is experienced enough to either clean up after themselves or not to leave any evidence in the first place."

Helen and Lorne nodded their agreement.

Sally scanned the area again and pointed at a camera over on the far side of the workshop. "Have you checked it?"

Covering her face with her hands, Helen tutted. "I'm sorry, I should have told you sooner. The twins showed me the footage when I first arrived. We've got the killer arriving and leaving, but that's as far as it goes. We can't make out if the person is male or female. The murderer was on the premises for a total of nineteen minutes."

"Interesting. Okay, if you've covered all the possibilities here then our next step would be to see what the neighbours have to say about the incident, except we're out in the sticks with no other properties in sight. Was that a key element for the killer to consider?" Sally suggested.

"More than likely," Lorne agreed.

"Therefore, with all the angles dealt with here, then there's only one place left for us to go. To have a word with the wife. I'm sorry, she's had long enough to get over the initial shock now. If she's eager for us to get on with the investigation then she should be willing to be interviewed. She needs to be made aware that every second matters when an investigation starts."

"I'm inclined to agree with you now I've had time to sit back and digest everything," Helen said. "Do you want me to give her a call, check if she's willing to see us?"

"No. I think we should show up at her door, pull the sympathy card and see if she's willing to speak with us," Sally stated. "I think we should still have a quick chat with the twins before we go, though."

"Shall I leave you to it? Just in case they open up to you more than they were prepared to do with me?"

"Might be a good idea. Why don't you wait in the car, Helen? We shouldn't be too long. I take it you have the wife's address?"

"I do. She lives ten minutes away. I'll be in the car. I have a few notes I need to go over while I have a few spare minutes."

Helen left the building, and Sally walked towards the office and knocked on the door. Lorne remained behind, checking the crime scene further, in case they'd overlooked anything.

"Hi, is it possible to have a word with you both?"

The two men were sitting side by side behind the desk going through the paperwork spread out in front of them.

"Please, come in. We'd rather speak to you than deal with this crap, it's mind-boggling. Neither of us could get our heads around it and preferred to leave it to the boss. Not sure what will happen to the place now he's no longer with us," Chris said.

"His wife is Kelly, isn't she?"

They both nodded.

"Do you think she'll sell up or choose to employ a manager to run the place for her instead?"

"Hard to say. She doesn't have much to do with this place,

we rarely see her," Sean said. "If I had to put money on it, I would plump for her selling up and washing her hands of the garage. That'll leave us in the shit, won't it, mate?"

"It will, but it's something we'll need to accept if her heart isn't in it."

"Do you get on well with her?" Sally sat in the only other chair available, and it wobbled beneath her.

"Sorry, do you want to swap with me? That one needs chucking out," Chris offered.

"It seems sturdy enough. As long as I'm aware of the wobble, I should be fine."

"You asked if we get on with her," Chris reminded her. "Hard to say, we don't really know her well enough. Never really had a conversation with her, just shouted hello on the odd occasion when she's shown up."

"How was their marriage?"

The twins glanced at each other and shrugged.

Sean said, "Andy seemed happy enough with her. I'm not saying he never complained about her, we all have our moments, don't we? But on the whole, I would be willing to put my neck on the line and say their marriage was okay."

"And you told my colleague, DI Edmonds, that none of the customers have ever had a gripe with Andy. Do you stand by that statement?"

Sean tutted. "We spoke about this after DI Edmonds left, and something came to mind, but it happened a few years ago when Andy first took over running the garage."

"Can you tell me what that was?"

"A bloke, can't even remember his name now, it was that long ago, he caused a bit of a stir when his car was delayed. He threatened to sue Andy for not sticking to his promise of when the car would be ready. Andy told him to do one and to never come back. That night, we had a few cars for sale on the forecourt, and all the tyres got slashed."

"Did the cameras pick up the culprit?"

Sean shook his head. "No, we didn't have any back then. Not long after, Andy decided to stop selling cars and he installed the cameras."

"And everything settled down after that, or were there further incidents that occurred?"

"No, that was the end of it. Andy vowed that day that he would never let another customer down, it wasn't worth the bloody hassle. He stuck to his word, too."

"Okay, one last thing before I go, is there a chance I can view the footage from the other day, specifically when the killer arrived and left?"

Chris stood and walked towards the door. "Yep, we can sort that out for you. I have already given a copy to DI Edmonds."

"I know. I just thought while I'm here I could take a quick peek at it."

"Do you want to come with me? The security equipment is set up in the other room."

Sally carefully left her chair and called out for Lorne to join her. "Are you free? I'm going to view the footage."

"I'll be right with you," Lorne called back and joined Chris and Sally in the storeroom. Things were so tight in there, Lorne had to hook her arm around Sally's waist to view the smallest of screens.

Chris ran the footage. He dipped his head back so they could get a clearer view of the screen.

"Blimey, the person seems cocksure, didn't anxiously look back over their shoulder, they just walked straight through the door," Sally stated.

"Are you sure you don't recognise the person, Chris?" Lorne asked.

"Not at all. We've both viewed the footage over and over

in the hope that something would ring a bell with us, but it didn't, sorry."

"What about the camera I saw inside the garage?" Sally asked.

Chris grimaced. "It's a fake one. Andy insisted putting it in as a deterrent in case any of the customers tried it on with him."

"Great," Sally murmured. "Had it been a real one that could have been the key to catching the killer."

"Sorry, nothing to do with me. Things like that were down to the boss, Sean and I just work here. Andy never asked us for advice about things that didn't concern us."

Sally touched his forearm. "No, it should be me apologising to you. I shouldn't have said anything. Don't worry, hopefully the forensic guys will be able to work their magic and enhance the image for us."

"That would be cool. Sean and I are desperate to know who the killer is. We keep wondering if we know the person, if they might be a customer and, if so, whether they will come back and hurt either of us."

"I wish I could offer you some kind of assurance that won't happen, but without knowing who the killer is or what their motive is, all I can advise you to do is remain vigilant and take extra precautions when you lock up at the end of the night, just in case."

"We said the same. I hope I don't regret telling you this, but we've taken extra precautions, hidden certain objects around the garage that we can use as weapons in the likelihood of us being attacked, you know, if either one of us is left on our own here."

"And I shouldn't be telling you that I think that's a good idea. Is there any chance of either of you being left alone during the day?"

"Sometimes a customer will ask us to drop a car off for them."

"I see. Between you and me, you should do what's necessary to protect yourselves, but don't forget, in an emergency you should always call nine-nine-nine."

"We'll bear that in mind. Was there anything else I can help you with?"

"No, I think we're done here now. Thanks for your time, and I'm sorry we had to meet under such dreadful circumstances."

"Me, too. I hope you catch the bastard who did this to Andy. He was one of the good guys, he didn't deserve to be murdered like that."

"I know. We're going to do our very best to find the person responsible, don't worry."

Helen led the way to Kelly Grant's house which was a detached cottage, situated at the end of a country lane. Nearby there were two other cottages, but other than that they were surrounded by fields.

"Wow, this is idyllic, isn't it?" Sally whistled.

"You could say that. Hey, you've got no right to feel envious, not when you live in that stunning manor house of yours."

"I know. No matter how much I love my home, it can feel a little austere at times. I'm probably talking out of my arse, but do you understand what I mean?"

"I do. Nonetheless, it's still a beautiful home. Tony and I love visiting 'our gentry neighbours'."

Sally playfully thumped Lorne in the thigh. "Get out of here. We're just us, down-to-earth Simon and Sal. Anyway, the home was Simon's to begin with. I moved my belongings in once he'd slipped a ring on my finger. Enough chatting, let's see if the wife is willing to speak with us now. I hope so, I'd hate to get heavy with her."

"Yeah, please take a step back for now. Perhaps she needed more time than others to get used to the idea of her husband never coming home again. There's the business to consider as well. Maybe she found it too overwhelming when Helen called to see her the other day."

"Yeah, you're right. We need to give her the benefit of the doubt. Are you ready?"

"Are you going to let Helen lead the way in the interview?"

"We'll see how it goes. She seems a little hit and miss to me. Or should I say, lacking in expcrience. The last thing we need is for her to screw it up for us."

"I like your thinking. Let her take the lead and you jump in if necessary."

Sally laughed. "If that's what I said."

They left the car and joined Helen on the narrow pavement outside the gate of the cottage.

"You neglected to tell us how beautiful this place is," Sally said.

"Sorry. I have no idea what it looks like inside, I didn't get over the threshold on my first visit. I don't mind telling you that I'm bricking it."

Sally smiled and offered, "Do you want me to take the lead? I don't mind."

"That would be great, Sally. I'm a bag of nerves for some reason. Never felt this way before. Maybe it's because she rejected me the first time around."

"It happens. You should try again. When I first joined the Force, I was always told by my mentor never to give up at the first hurdle."

"Unfortunately, mine only stayed with me for a week, to teach me the ropes quickly, and then she retired."

"Ouch, not ideal. Don't worry, I've got this. Let's turn it into a watch-and-learn exercise, okay?"

"You're brilliant, you both are, for taking me under your wings like this. I can't tell you how much I appreciate it."

Sally waved her words away and opened the wooden gate that led them into the equally stunning garden, which wrapped around the house. On either side of the path was a patch of lawn surrounded by a variety of cottage plants that gently swayed in the breeze. Sally rang the bell and removed her warrant card from her jacket pocket.

The door was opened by a young girl, no older than sixteen. "Yes. Can I help?"

"Hi, I'm DI Sally Parker, and these ladies are DS Lorne Warner and DI Helen Edmonds. Is it possible to speak with Mrs Grant, please?"

"Is this about what happened to Dad?" the girl asked, her voice catching in her throat.

"Yes. Is she okay to speak with us now? DI Edmonds called to see her before, but your mother wasn't up to speaking with her at the time."

"I think she's feeling better today. Although I have to tell you, the doctor has given her some medication to help her sleep, and I think it's making her super emotional."

"That's understandable. And you are?"

"I'm Melissa Grant." She opened the door and took a step back into the hallway. "Can I ask you to remove your shoes? Only Mum's very particular, and we have a cream carpet in the lounge."

"Not a problem."

The three of them removed their shoes, and then Melissa took them into the lounge without warning her mother that they had arrived and wanted to speak with her. Sally braced herself for fireworks but was surprised when Kelly welcomed them and invited them to take a seat. Sally's eye was immediately drawn to the beams and the inglenook fireplace in the beautifully decorated room. She could also tell that Kelly had a penchant for Laura Ashley designs. They were recognisable in the curtains, blinds and the cushions enhancing the grey fabric sofas.

Kelly turned to Helen and apologised. "I'm so sorry I sent you packing the other day. I simply couldn't handle you pounding me with questions, not when my head was spinning and my heart was breaking. I must warn you, I'm still very tearful, and the doctor has put me on medication that is toying with my emotions."

"There's no need to apologise," Helen said. "We're not here to make your life unbearable, we promise. All we're trying to do is find out what you know about your husband's death."

"How would I know? I wasn't there when it happened," Kelly replied, her brow twisting into a frown.

Sally glanced at Helen, silently asking her permission to take over as they'd agreed outside. Helen gave a slight nod.

"What DI Edmonds meant was we need to know if your husband has ever discussed either falling out with any friends or neighbours leading up to his death."

"What neighbours? There are only two of them and they're both widows. So, if you're thinking one of them might have killed him, you must be out of your minds. As for friends, we only have a few left. Since Andy took over the garage, we haven't had the chance to go out much or to entertain, not like we used to. Friends tend to fall by the wayside when we don't reciprocate or take up invitations to parties et cetera. He was that determined to make a success of the garage, he spent most of his time there, didn't he, love?" Kelly asked her daughter.

"Yes. We didn't see a lot of Dad. We used to a while back, but not lately."

Sally nodded. "I have to ask, did that put a strain on your marriage, Kelly?"

"You'd think it would, but surprisingly it didn't. I was quite happy to be with the girls. I have twins, Melissa and Victoria, she's out at the moment. She went back to college, but Melissa decided to stay at home with me. She's been struggling to understand her father's death as much as I have." Kelly reached for her daughter's hand and grasped it.

"It's been hard for all of us, though," Melissa added. "He was our dad, and we miss him."

"We do, love. It's taken us a while to get used to the idea that we're never going to see him again." Kelly turned her attention back to Sally. "Do you have any idea who did this to him, or why?"

"Not at the moment. We've viewed the footage from the garage, but it's not the clearest of images. We saw the killer arrive and leave but nothing in between."

"That's because Andy was a cheapskate. He bought the cheapest equipment he could lay his hands on at the time. I told him he'd probably live to regret it..." Kelly paused to swallow down the emotions welling up. "And I was right, wasn't I? There are times when you hate being right, this is one of them." She shook her head, and the tears surfaced and splashed onto her cheek.

Melissa handed her mother a tissue. "Come on, Mum. We promised each other we would try to stay strong today."

Kelly touched her daughter's cheek. "I know, and look how long that lasted. It's so hard for me right now, love. Your father was the only man I have ever loved, and now he's gone. I feel nothing but despair. Not only do I have his funeral to arrange when I'm consumed with grief, but there's also the business to consider as well. It all keeps overwhelming me in waves, and I don't know how I'm going to get past it."

"I'm trying to help you as much as I can, Mum, but you're not the only one struggling." Melissa cried, too.

They hugged each other, and Sally's heart went out to both of them.

"We appreciate this is a very difficult time for you. If there's anything we can do to help, you only have to ask."

Kelly released her daughter and nodded. She wiped her eyes on one tissue and blew her nose on another. "Thank you, we really appreciate your kindness. I think it's something we need to work through as a family."

"Do you have any siblings or other members of your family living close by who could lend a hand?"

"Not really. I'm aware they all have their own lives to lead. The girls have been brilliant, especially Victoria, she's gone back to college today but has been cooking all our meals since…"

"I'm glad you're surrounded by people who love you. When it comes to sorting out the funeral, I can assure you, the undertaker will give you all the help and assurance you need that things will go right. I would suggest taking their advice on board unless there was anything specific your husband wanted for his funeral."

Kelly stared at Sally. "No, we never even discussed funeral arrangements. He was forty, for God's sake. Neither of us ever anticipated our lives being cut short."

"I can understand that. Again, if you need any help, we're here for you."

"Thank you. So what happens next? Do you know when his body will be released?"

"I'll have a word with the pathologist. I'll get her to give you a call. She can go through the process with you, if that would help?"

"It would. It's the not knowing. I usually Google everything, but not this time. I think it would be too confusing for me."

"Perhaps. I hate to ask, but did your husband ever borrow any money off anyone?"

Kelly blinked and shook her head. "No, not as far as I know. Why would you ask that question?"

"It's a line of enquiry we have to cover when it's unclear why someone has been murdered."

"No. We own the house outright, and the business has always made a profit from day one, so he would have had no reason to borrow money. God, I've just twigged, you're talking about either drugs or a loan shark, aren't you?"

"No way!" Melissa shouted. "My dad would never get involved with anything dodgy like that. He loved his family and would never put us at risk."

"I'm glad to hear it, forgive me for asking. It's just, at the moment, the evidence and clues as to who the killer might be are scarce. I suppose I'm guilty of clutching at straws."

"Clutch away. I'm at a loss to know what to tell you. Andy was a good man, an excellent father to my two girls and the best husband he could possibly be to me. He was hard-working and a fantastic provider for our family. We wanted for nothing. He paid the mortgage off by the time he was thirty-five, which was his ambition when we got married at twenty. I couldn't have asked for a better partner, and now… he's gone and I don't know why. Please, you have to find who killed him. I need to know why they've robbed my family of such a lovely man."

"We're going to do our very best. I don't want to bombard you with details today, but although DI Edmonds, Helen, is in charge of your case, we're here to assist her as we've been dealing with a similar case."

"Similar case? What does that mean? Please tell me what you know, I can take it."

Sally ran through the details of the cold case and watched the colour drain from Kelly's face.

"Wow, how can that happen? You said the culprit was banged up, forgive my confusion."

"Not at all. We've decided to work together to see if we can make any sense of it. I have to ask, did either you or your husband know the other victim, Denis Short?"

She stared at the carpet in front of Sally and after a while shook her head. "No, I don't think so. Who was he?"

"A school caretaker in Acle."

"No, definitely not. I know that's not going to help you."

"Don't worry. I'm sure a major clue will come our way soon. What I want to do before we leave is assure you that we're going to do our very best for your family. Helen and I will leave you a card. Feel free to reach out to either one of us with any questions you may have."

"I have a couple. How long will it be before you catch someone? And what kind of punishment can they expect?"

Sally sucked in a breath. "Hard to say how long it's going to take us to bring the culprit to justice. As to what punishment they will receive, that will be down to the judge. The perpetrator will be charged with murder, which can carry a whole life sentence."

"But not always," Melissa said.

"No, unfortunately that's true," Sally agreed. "I wish it wasn't, but there can be extenuating circumstances to consider in certain cases. That won't be the case where Andy's death is concerned, though, I can assure you."

"Good. Whoever killed him needs to face the consequences of their actions and be punished accordingly," Kelly said. "In my opinion, the worst thing this country did was abolish the death sentence. There's no deterrent these days."

Sally nodded. "I know I shouldn't say this, but I wholeheartedly agree with you. The lack of genuine deterrents has made our jobs so much harder over the years. But those words didn't come from my lips."

Nodding, Kelly smiled. "I can sense the frustration the police feel when they see criminals getting away with minimal sentences."

"You're not wrong. Still, we will continue to give it our all, see if that can change the system in the future. I doubt it, but we live in hope. Is there anything else you need to ask before we go?"

"No, I don't think so. I have confidence in you as a team." She faced Helen and added, "I'm so sorry I turned you away the other day, my head wasn't in the right place to deal with answering any of your questions. I realise how wrong I was now."

Helen smiled. "Not at all. Everyone has to deal with grief in their own way. There's never a one-size-fits-all package we can supply to help you through the process. I'm glad you have your daughters with you at this time. And, I'd just like to reinforce what DI Parker has told you, we're here if you need us, day or night. You also have my assurance that we're going to give this investigation our all. At the end of the day, it will be in everyone's best interests to get this killer off the streets and behind bars as soon as possible."

"Thank you. Sorry, how rude of me, I didn't even offer you a drink when you arrived. Please don't hold that against me."

They all laughed.

"We won't," Sally told her. "Well, if there's nothing else, we're going to leave you to it. I'll contact the pathologist and ask her to give you a call later today, if that's okay with you?"

"It is. Thank you. As soon as I've spoken with her, I'll get in touch with a couple of funeral homes. Having this conversation with you has given me the strength to sort out what needs to be done going forward now. I can't thank you enough for that."

She stood and showed them to the front door. Sally, Lorne and Helen all slipped either their shoes or boots back on and stepped outside the house.

"Thank you again for your kindness and compassion."

"You're welcome," Sally replied.

"Take care of yourself," Helen said.

The three of them walked up the path to the cars.

"Where do we go from here?" Helen asked.

"Do you want to give Pauline a call?" Sally asked.

"Yes, I can do that. Sorry, I meant what should happen with the case now. Would it be better if I worked out of your office, with you?"

Sally contemplated her question for a second or two. "Yes, that seems like the best idea. You might want to run it past your chief first."

"I'm sure she won't mind. I'll ring the pathologist first and then my boss."

"We'll split it. I'll give Pauline a call, how's that?"

"Thanks, maybe that would be for the best."

They jumped back into their respective cars and made the calls then, after receiving the thumbs-up from Helen, they set off back to the station. Pauline hadn't been available to take Sally's call, so she'd asked one of the techs to pass on a message for Pauline to phone Kelly once Andy's body had been dealt with. Whether that meant his wife would want to visit would be up to Kelly to decide.

AFTER PICKING up a mixture of sandwiches and cakes for the team, they headed back to the station. DCI Cummings had granted permission for Helen to join Sally's team on a temporary basis, and the three of them, once lunch was out of the way, decided that a call to the governor of Norwich Prison should be a priority.

Sally made the call and put the phone on speaker. Ken Pike was more than willing to talk to them. Sally explained the situation about having a second murder to investigate alongside Helen. Ken was shocked into silence.

"Mr Pike, Ken, are you still with us?"

"Yes, sorry, forgive me, I'm still here. I'm stunned to hear such news. How can that be possible?"

"Well, between us, we've come up with the possibility that we might be dealing with a copycat killer."

"What? Oh my, surely not?"

"We're open to suggestions if you can think of something we haven't considered."

"Me? No, sorry, I haven't got anything for you. Goodness, I've heard of such things, of course I have, but I have to tell you that I've never experienced anything like this in my ten years in the service. Is there anything I can do to help?"

"I'm glad you asked. Has Wallace shared a cell with anyone since he was sentenced?"

"No, never. He asked for a single cell. At the time of his arrival we had one available, and he's been in it ever since."

Sally grimaced, and Lorne scribbled something down on a piece of paper.

Sally wagged a finger. "Just say it out loud, Lorne. Ken is aware you and Helen are both listening."

"Oh, yes, silly me," Lorne said. "What about any prisoners who have been released in the last week or so, are there any?"

"Can you hang tight while I check the system?"

"Go for it," Sally said.

Keys tapped, and Ken mumbled a few expletives. "Sorry for the swearing, this damn computer has been the bane of my life all week, it's so ruddy slow. Ah, here it is, I've given it a kick under the table."

"They all need that now and again." Sally laughed. "Any luck?"

"Yes, we've got a Carl Harper and Benjamin Ash, both released on the same day, Tuesday of this week."

"I suppose my next question should be, were they close to Wallace while they were inside?"

"I'd have to ask the rest of the staff about that. Can I get back to you in about half an hour?"

"Sure, thanks. Also, while you're still with us, can you also check if Wallace has received any visitors lately?"

"I'll check the register and call you back. TTFN," he said brightly.

Sally ended the call and sat back.

"He seems a nice man," Helen said.

"He is. When Lorne and I went to visit the prisoner the other day, Ken came to see us upon our arrival. A very amenable chap, which is why I had no hesitation in calling him. Let's hope he can come up with the goods for us, because if he can't supply us with any clues then we're stumped."

Lorne sighed. "I agree, unless the lab can enhance the image of the killer for us."

"I hate being reliant on other people to come up with the answers. Why don't we search for Carl Harper and Benjamin Ash in the meantime?"

"I'll do that if you like," Helen volunteered. She winked and added, "I've got a friend who is a probation officer. She owes me a favour or two, I'll call them in."

"Fantastic."

Helen stepped out of the office to ring her friend.

Sally tried to clear a number of her emails while Lorne dealt with some of the brown letters in her in-tray. There was no point either of them doing anything else while they waited for Ken to phone back.

Helen, fizzing with excitement, entered the office again. "Knock, knock. All right if I join you?"

"You don't have to knock." Sally gestured for Helen to take a seat. "What have you got for us?"

"Two addresses. The men were put at different locations. Well, separate guest houses but a few doors apart."

"That's handy. We'll wait for Ken to get back to us and then shoot out to pay them both a visit."

"Sounds good to me," Helen agreed.

With that, the phone rang. It was Ken Pike.

"Hi, Ken, what do you have for us? You're on speaker with Lorne and Helen present again."

"Hi, ladies. I might have something interesting for you. I wasn't aware that Wallace had visitors, but in the last couple of weeks a Stan Lawrence has visited him a few times."

"Interesting," Sally replied. "I don't suppose you'd know why he would visit Wallace all of a sudden?"

"No idea, sorry."

"It doesn't matter. We'll visit him and ask the question ourselves. What about the other prisoners? Has Wallace been interacting with anyone else lately?"

"I asked my head officer, and he told me he didn't know as he doesn't keep an eye on a particular prisoner twenty-four-seven, so anything is possible."

"Okay, that's great. If we need anything else, can I give you a call?"

"My line or my door is always open for you, Inspector. Good luck with your enquiries."

"Thanks, we're going to need it." Sally ended the call.

"What do you suggest we do next?" Lorne asked.

Helen sat forward, eagerly awaiting the answer.

"Well, I think as we have the address for Harper and Ash, we should pay them a visit."

"And what about Lawrence?" Helen asked.

"We'll get the team to try and hunt down an address for him, and once we have that to hand, we'll nip round and see him as well."

The three of them finished their drinks and, on the way back through the outer office, Sally brought the team up to date with what they'd learned and asked them to trace Lawrence for them in their absence.

"And when we find him, what then?" Jordan asked.

"Ring me and we'll visit him while we're out." Sally got the impression that the rest of the team were a little restless. Maybe that was to do with Helen being involved in the investigation now, or perhaps she was guilty of reading something into it that simply wasn't there. "Work quickly, guys. Let's nail this bastard to the wall before he gets the chance to choose another victim."

SALLY AND LORNE set off in one car, and Helen decided to take her car as well, which made sense. They arrived at the first B&B. Helen took that one while Sally and Lorne called at the second one. Both properties were brightly painted, white walls and either yellow or orange windowsills. The landlady at the second address told Sally that Benjamin Ash had gone out for the day.

"Do you know where?"

Mrs Powell wasn't sure. "I'm sorry, I'm not the type of person who keeps tabs on her guests day and night. As long as they pay for their rooms, that's all I'm bothered about."

"I understand. Thanks for your help."

They left the property and walked up the road to join Helen. She was coming up the path of the B&B where Harper was staying. Helen looked as dejected as Sally felt.

"I take it he wasn't in."

"No and the landlady couldn't tell me where he was either. How did you get on?"

"Pretty much the same." Sally scanned the area and pointed up the road. "There's a café up there. Why don't we hang around here for a while, see if they return? We can keep an eye out for them over a cup of coffee."

"Sounds good to me," Lorne backed her up.

"And me. This one is on me, ladies. You refused to take anything for my sandwich earlier."

"If you insist," Sally said.

They set off up the quiet road.

"I'm going to get on to Joanna, ask her to send us a photo of Harper and Ash, otherwise we won't know who to keep an eye open for," Lorne said.

"Good idea. I knew I brought you along for a reason."

Lorne playfully thumped Sally's upper arm. "You'll pay for that comment."

Sally grinned. "Not today I won't, this one is on Helen."

Lorne rolled her eyes and rang the station as they relocated to the café. "All done. She's going to send the photos through once she's sourced them."

They entered the small café.

"What would you like?" Helen asked.

"Flat white for me," Sally replied.

"Ditto for me," Lorne said.

"Take a seat, I'll place the order."

As soon as they were seated by the window giving them the best view of the B&Bs, Lorne's phone pinged with a text message. She opened it and forwarded the two photos Joanna had sent to Sally. "Coming your way."

Sally removed her phone from her pocket and placed it on the table beside her. "Got them. They seem pretty young, both of them."

Helen joined them and sat next to Sally. Helen had a nosy at the photos. "What are young men of that age doing with their lives? They can't be any more than twenty-two, can they?"

Sally shrugged. "Could be any number of reasons why they've got into trouble. Statistics tell us the chances of them reoffending is pretty high, too, unless someone in the probation service is willing to go the extra mile and help them adjust to the outside world."

"I agree, they need a purpose in life that will keep them out of trouble," Helen said. "My friend, Bonnie, has both lads on her books. She's got a good record for helping boys of this age to readjust to the outside. Once they're put away, some of them are cruelly disowned by their families. That can be the beginning of the decline for some. Most men I know will shrug it off and get on with their lives. Not so easy when you feel society is against you like these guys might feel."

"Like I said, we don't know their specific stories so it would be wrong for us to make any assumptions. From experience—and this isn't a dig at your friend, Bonnie, who is doing her best to make a difference—once young men step outside the prison, the only life they know is how to wheel and deal, and they haven't got an alternative in place, hence the reason why they tend to reoffend and often end up back inside."

"Heartbreaking as it is," Lorne said, "I suppose it's like everything, the funds just aren't there for the probation service in order for them to make a difference."

"I agree. Bonnie said her department is dealing with cutbacks on a yearly basis, which is no help to anyone, least of all the young men who are willing to turn their lives around but feel shafted when they get out of prison," Helen stated.

The waitress brought their drinks over and handed them around. "The latte is this one."

"That's mine, my friends ordered the two flat whites," Helen said and smiled at the young woman.

The waitress walked back to the counter.

"How long are we going to be prepared to wait for?" Helen asked.

Sally tore off the ends of two packets of sugar and poured them into her coffee. "No more than an hour. Hopefully, by then the rest of the team will have sourced an address for Lawrence, so if we don't have any joy here, we can jog over to his place and have a word with him."

"Hey, my jogging days are over." Lorne snorted.

"Why don't you tell us a bit about yourself, Helen?" Sally asked.

"You'll get bored pretty quickly, there's not really that much to tell."

"Give it a go, we'll be the judge of that," Sally insisted.

"I was brought up in Norwich. My parents separated when I was in my teens. I've got a brother I can't stand. He's always begging me for money I don't have instead of getting off his backside and getting a job. He says I owe him as our parents favoured me when we were growing up. He's talking bullshit, they didn't, but he's not prepared to listen. So last year, I told him never to contact me again. Harsh, and you'll probably think badly of me, but since he's been out of my life, I've been far happier."

"That's great. It doesn't do anyone any good to have toxic people in their lives. Do you still see your parents?"

"My mum, yes, weekly. She's nearly sixty now and tells me repeatedly that she's feeling her age. I've told her to see the doctor because it could be down to the menopause."

"I can vouch for that," Lorne said. "I went through the same thing a few months ago until Sally pushed me to see the doctor for advice. He put me on HRT, and I haven't looked back. My husband, Tony, appreciates the change in my mood as well. Are you married, Helen?"

"I'm engaged. I live with Ralph but I'm not sure it's going to work out. He was my first real boyfriend, and I jumped at the chance to leave home. I think I'm regretting that decision now. He's changed so much since I moved in with him. We both work, but when I get home at night, he expects me to cook every meal, do the washing and ironing plus all the cleaning. I think he wants another mother, not a girlfriend or wife."

"Christ, I'd nip that in the bud as soon as I could," Sally said. "Lorne and I are very lucky with our husbands. Our marriages are both partnerships. It's fifty-fifty in our homes, isn't it, Lorne?"

"Totally. Although I know what you mean about men expecting us to live up to what their mothers do for them, I had that with my ex-husband. I was exhausted by the end of the week. He couldn't even cook beans on toast. I tried teaching him and it was an utter disaster, so I gave up. I'm sure some men cock up a chore they've been given on purpose, so we don't ask them to do it again in the future. Tony is the total opposite. We run a kennel together. He puts the same effort into dealing with that and looking after the chores around the house as I do, even though he's classed as disabled, although you wouldn't know he's only got one leg if you met him."

"Wow, really? He sounds amazing and would probably put most men to shame. Would your advice be for me to dump Ralph? I've been contemplating it for months, but I've never had the courage to start the conversation."

Sally inhaled a breath. "Only you can decide whether it will be worth continuing with your relationship or not. Have you tried discussing the issues that are annoying you with Ralph?"

Helen took a sip from her coffee. "No, I've tried to a couple of times, but I always dry up. He's got a bit of a temper, and I'm not sure what he'll do if I put my foot down."

Lorne shook her head. "My advice would be to get out. My ex turned violent. He only hit me a couple of times before I said enough was enough."

"And I suppose you know all about my relationship with my ex?" Sally asked.

Helen cringed. "I've heard the rumours. I wasn't sure if they were true or not. He was put in prison for… assaulting you, wasn't he?"

"Raping me on several occasions. Honestly, he lived behind a mask for years. He was a pilot for BA, flew all over the world, but he became a monster the second he came home. I put up with him using me as a punchbag for years until I took a good look at myself in the mirror one day and announced, 'I'm done with this'."

"I'm so sorry you had to go through that, Sally. Can I ask how you learnt to trust your second husband?"

"I thought it would be difficult, but it was easy in the end. We knew each other professionally before we started dating, which helped. He was the former pathologist for the area. We went out on a few dates, and that was it. Before long I was moving out of my parents' home and into his swanky manor house with him. Don't get me wrong, he has his moments, but his moods are minor, and they don't last long when he gets them. What's more, he never takes it out on me, not like my ex."

"Men, who'd have them, eh?" Helen sniggered.

"Women need to stand their ground more and not let men walk all over them like they did in our grandmothers' days. Times were different back then. Most women didn't hold down a full-time job, it was up to them to look after the home. But times have changed, and men need to step up to the plate and acknowledge that. I think a majority of them do nowadays, like Tony and Simon, but there are others who continue to live in the past," Lorne said.

Something caught Sally's eye. She pointed out of the window at two young men standing outside the closest B&B they had tried earlier. "Okay, ladies, I think this is it. Drink up and we'll make our move."

"Shall we question the men together or split up?" Helen asked, an edge of wariness to her tone.

"Together, I think that would be for the best."

They left the café and marched down the street until they came to the first B&B where Benjamin Ash was staying. Sally asked the landlady she'd already spoken to if they could have a word with Ash.

"I can ask. Let me ring his room." She picked up the phone on the desk beside her. "Mr Ash, yes, there are three ladies down here to see you... we'll see you soon then." She hung up and said, "He's on his way down."

They waited at the bottom of the stairs for the young man.

He saw them and paused mid-step. "What do you want? You're cops, aren't you? I can smell you a mile off."

Sally produced her warrant card. "We are. You haven't done anything wrong, we're only here to ask you a few questions."

"Well, if I ain't done nothing wrong you can do one. You can't come around here, hounding me because I've only just got out of the nick."

"Honestly, there's nothing to it. We have a few questions to ask you about an investigation we're working on."

"Ha, I've heard that before, and why are there three of you?"

"It's a joint investigation. No tricks, this is purely legitimate, I promise."

His gaze flicked between them all. "I want to see all your badges or I'm going back upstairs. I'm sensing this is a trap."

Lorne and Helen showed him their IDs.

"I swear, it's not a trap. A few questions and we'll leave you alone," Sally assured him.

She could see the hesitancy in his eyes. He spread his arms out to the sides. "Okay, you win. Any funny business and I'll report you, you got that?"

"There won't be, don't worry."

He continued walking down the stairs.

The landlady whispered, "I don't want any trouble, ladies. You can go through to the lounge, it's the door behind you."

"Thanks, and there won't be. We just want to have a chat with him," Helen said.

Sally turned and entered the lounge which was set out like a nursing home. She stood in the centre of the room and faced Ash when he came in. Lorne and Helen stood either side of Sally.

"All right, I'm here, what's this all about?" Ash demanded.

"Do you want to take a seat?"

"No, say what you've got to say and let me get on with my day and my life."

"It's about your time in prison," Sally began. "We were wondering if you had anything to do with Bob Wallace while you were in there."

"What? Are you kidding me? Why would I have anything to do with that bastard? He's a serial killer."

"We know what he is. Are you sure?" Sally asked.

He flung his arms out to the sides again. "I said so, didn't I? What, is my word not good enough for you?"

"Yes, I'm sorry. No offence."

"Plenty taken," he retaliated. "Is that it?"

"One last question, if I may?"

"Get on with it," Ash snapped.

"Did you see anyone hanging around with Wallace on the inside?"

"No. He was a loner. Not many prisoners I know want to spend their time with a nutjob like that."

"Okay, that's all we needed to know. You're free to go."

"Thank fuck for that. Bloody coppers, once you've got a record, you never leave us alone, do you?" He stormed out of the room, not bothering to wait for Sally to answer.

"On to the next one, let's hope he's not as angry." Sally led the way out of the B&B.

Helen thanked the landlady for her time on the way out. They walked fifteen metres to the next B&B and went through the same process.

The landlady again insisted she didn't want any trouble, and after Sally assured her that wouldn't be the case, the woman rang Harper's room. He told them he'd be down in a minute but never appeared.

The landlady showed them up to his room and knocked on the door. There was no response, so Sally asked her to use the master key to gain access to the room. When the landlady reluctantly opened the door, they found the room empty, but the window was wide open. Lorne shot across the room.

"He's making his way up the alley now."

The three of them ran back downstairs and sprinted around the corner to the back of the property. Harper was leisurely walking towards them.

Sally smiled and showed her ID. "Going somewhere, were you, Mr Harper?"

"Fuck off, leave me alone. I knew this would happen. I've been out of the nick barely two days and already the coppers are knocking at my door."

Sally held her hands up. "If you'll give us a chance to explain why we've come to see you, all this can be over and done with in a couple of minutes."

He folded his arms and leaned against the fence alongside him. "Go on then, let's get this over with."

"All we wanted to ask you is if you'd had any dealings with Bob Wallace when you were inside."

"That tosser? No way. I was told to steer clear of him the day I arrived. I appreciated the warning. The guy gave me the sodding creeps."

"Did anyone hang around with him?"

"Not that I noticed. Everyone felt the same about him, none of us trusted the fucker. I'd heard he'd slashed a guy's throat not long after he'd been banged up. I had no intention of asking him if that was true or not."

"Okay, that's all we needed to know. See, it wasn't so bad, was it?" Sally smiled.

"Why do you want to know?" Harper asked, his eyes narrowing.

"Just making enquiries as part of an investigation we're working on."

"What, the three of you? And they say there are not enough coppers to man the streets these days. That's a laugh."

"Thanks for your time. I might suggest you use the front door to return to your room, less chance of you breaking your neck."

"Screw you, lady. I'll do what I want, not what some stuck-up copper tells me to do." He left the alley ahead of them.

"Effing tosser," Sally whispered. She stared after him and jumped when her phone rang. "Shit! Scared the crap out of me." She fished it out of her pocket. "Hi, Joanna, what have you got for us?"

"We've managed to locate Lawrence's address, boss."

"Thanks, we're out of the car right now, can you send it to me?"

"Will ping it across now. Good luck."

"Thanks, we're not having the best of that so far today. Just to bring you up to date, we've had a word with both ex-prisoners and, while they were talkative, they told us that they didn't go near Wallace on the inside and added that no one did. Apparently, he slit another prisoner's throat not long after his arrival. I think that served as a deterrent for the others not to go anywhere near him. He was also in a single cell. Which leads me to believe we might be barking up the wrong tree. Hopefully, speaking to Lawrence will put us back on the right track again, because at the moment, we're more than a little dejected about where this investigation is leading us."

"I get that, ma'am. We're doing our best back here in the hope that something else surfaces, but we're scuppered if nothing comes from the image at the garage."

Sally continued the walk back to the car and puffed out her cheeks when she reached the end of the alley. "Depending on how the time goes, I might pop into the lab on our way back, impress upon them how urgent it is for them to give us something we can use to move the investigation to a swift conclusion before someone else dies."

"Thanks, boss."

"See you later." She ended the call and pressed the key fob to open the car. "Do you want to follow us this time, Helen?"

"Makes sense. Is it far?"

"Back towards the station in Wymondham."

"Lead the way."

CHAPTER 7

In Sally's opinion, the low-rise block of flats either needed a major overhaul or razing to the ground. She'd passed this particular building and thought that many a time, but it was still standing and, by all accounts, was full of desperate families the council had let down over the years. "What a bloody choice, either live here or take your chances on the streets. Makes you wonder if the people working for the council know what they're doing, right?"

Lorne shuddered and exited the car that Sally had parked a fair distance from the property, just in case. "Makes you sick to think there are places like this still in existence. It is the same down in London. We had a fair number of deprived areas that I reckon the council had purposely forgotten about."

"Disgusting. Still, it's not our problem. I wonder how many councillors have said that over the years when they've held a meeting about this place."

Helen shut her car door and approached them. "It's the pits, isn't it? I had to come out here to a drug addict only last week. I don't mind telling you, when you sent me the address I nearly backed out."

Sally smiled. "Had I known we were coming to this very building, I think I would have done the same. It wasn't until we pulled up that I realised. Okay, that's all of our griping out of the way, let's go see what Lawrence is willing to tell us."

As they walked closer to the building, the smell hit them. Urine, faeces, vomit, stale food and more, all rolled into one, giving off the foulest of stenches. Sally pulled up a mask they'd been forced to wear for safety reasons during the pandemic and covered her nose.

"I don't suppose you've got a spare couple lingering in your pocket, have you?" Lorne asked, her voice muffled by her hand cupping over her mouth and nose.

"Sorry, you're out of luck."

Helen ran back to her car and returned carrying two masks, one of which she handed to Lorne.

"Cheers, Helen, that's very thoughtful, thank you."

"Creep," Sally muttered and turned to walk up the concrete stairwell that would lead them up to the second floor. "I suppose we should be grateful his flat is only two flights up. I think if it had been more, we'd be gagging for breath and would be forced to suffer the consequences."

"Definitely a blessing in disguise," Lorne agreed. She fiddled with her mask that was too big, shortening the ties at the side for a snug fit.

Sally used her jacket to cover her hand and knocked on the door. It took a while, but eventually a tall, slim, unkempt man opened it and stared at each of them in turn.

Sally held up her ID and announced, "DI Sally Parker, DS Lorne Warner and DI Helen Edmonds."

Lawrence eyed Sally from head to foot. "Yeah, what do you want, another badge for bravely telling me your names or setting foot on this estate?" He sniggered at his own inane joke.

"We'd like to come in and have a chat with you, if that's all right, Mr Lawrence?"

"About what? I ain't done nothing wrong. I mind my own business most days, I suggest you do the same. Your lot ain't welcome around here. I hope you had the common sense to park on the other side of the estate, if not, you're risking your tyres being slashed, or worse still, nicked. Cop cars always stand out a mile around here."

"Don't worry about us, we're aware of the problems in this area. Are you going to let us in?"

"Nope. Next question?" He leaned against the doorframe, folded his arms, and then watched, amused, as his spittle landed on the floor two inches from Sally's new boots.

"You're not doing yourself any favours, Mr Lawrence," she warned.

"Let's get one thing straight, shall we? I didn't invite the frigging cops to show up at my door. So, who's in the wrong, me or you?"

"No one. All we need to do is ask you a few questions and then we'll be on our way."

"Go on then. Just because you're gonna ask them, it doesn't mean I have to answer them, does it?" He grinned, his teeth, what he had left of them, stained from nicotine.

Sally glanced to the side of him rather than analyse the remains of food settled in the cracks of his teeth. He was vile, pure and simple, but nothing a good clean wouldn't put right, so why didn't he do it? No running hot water? Unlikely these days. "We believe you've recently started visiting Bob Wallace in Norwich prison. Can you tell us why?"

Beside her, Lorne extracted her notebook and pen.

He laughed, giving them another unwanted view of his

uncared-for teeth. "Ha, you won't be needing that, 'cos I ain't got nothing to say. Ask all you want, I ain't going to give you no answers."

Sally smiled and shrugged. "We can either do this the easy or hard way. The easy way would be here, with you respectfully responding to our questions, or the hard way would be to carry out this interview down at the station."

"Fuck off. You can't do that. I know my rights."

"And we have rights, too. We're investigating two serious crimes that have been committed and we have reason to believe you know something about both of those crimes."

"Bollocks. This is you lot talking shit and trying to fit me up again, ain't it? I don't know anying. I've been nowhere for weeks, so don't think you can go pinning any crimes on me, lady."

"It's inspector, and you're lying. We know that for a fact, because you visited Wallace in prison."

"All right, I meant apart from that. That was out of necessity."

Sally inclined her head. "Which was…?"

"That's for me and Bob to know."

"I have to inform you that my patience is wearing thin, Mr Lawrence. You've got two minutes to tell me why you visited the prison or I'm going to arrest you for perverting the course of justice."

He launched himself off the doorframe and glared at her. "You're talking out of your arse. Mind you, I'm not surprised, that's all coppers fucking do anyway, ain't it?"

"Not this copper. I'm warning you, either you answer my question within two minutes, or I'll call for backup and get them to escort you to the station where I will conduct the interview under caution. The choice is yours."

"Screw you. You can't show up here, tossing your threats

around. I'm an innocent man and I have frigging rights," he reminded her.

"Here's the thing, during a murder inquiry, so do we."

His face screwed up, and he shook his head a couple of times as if to wake his brain up. "What? Who's been murdered?"

"We have two victims, so take your pick. We believe they're connected. So, are you going to tell us why you have started visiting Wallace after all these years?"

"Wouldn't you like to know?"

Sally heaved out a sigh and faced Lorne. "Make the call. Might as well ask for an Armed Response Team to come. Tell them that a suspect is refusing to come to the station with us and he's armed and dangerous."

"That's a fucking lie, only to be expected from your mob. I know you're winding me up, that you've got nothing on me other than visiting an old pal of mine. Like I've already told you, I know my fucking rights."

Lorne made the call. Sally knew her partner was pretending. Lorne played her part, stepped away from the door and turned her back on Lawrence.

He craned his neck to try and hear what Lorne was saying.

Lorne ended her imaginary call and announced, "They'll be here in five minutes. They've just finished another job two streets away."

"What the fuck? You can't do this. If they lay one hand on me…" Lawrence objected.

Sally held up her hands. "There's an easy solution to that, start talking."

"I don't know anything. I visited a mate in nick, so what?"

"Why? There must be a reason for you suddenly visiting him. Tell us what it is."

"You're nuts. I don't have to tell you nothing about my

private conversations. So screw you, lady. Not that I would, I've got more sense than try it on with a copper. Filth by name and filth by nature, ain't ya?"

Sally ignored the rude comment and folded her arms. "Tell us why you visited the prison. The clock is ticking. You really don't want me to pass over the baton to the ART when they arrive, the outcome is never a good one."

"Fuck off. I don't know nothing, and you can't make me talk, despite flinging constant threats at me. All I did was visit him, end of."

"Except it's not the end, because after your visit one of our victims was found."

He held his hands up in front of him. "That's got nothing to do with me. You're trying to fit me up, and I ain't having it."

"Far from it. All we're trying to understand is why you have started visiting Wallace in prison."

"Because I have. Is there a bloody law against that? If there is, I wasn't aware, and neither was he."

"No, there's no law against it, but when a victim is found with the same MO as a serial killer's victims, but that killer has been inside for four years, then you can understand why we're here, can't you?"

"No, not at all. It's a coincidence."

Sally got the impression that the news about the victim hadn't come as a surprise to Lawrence. "Here's the thing, I don't know a copper still doing this job who has ever believed in coincidences. Do you want to give it another shot?"

"Not particularly."

He grinned, and again, Sally averted her eyes. This time she peered over her shoulder and winked at Helen and Lorne.

"I wonder how long the ART are going to be."

"Do you want me to chase it up, boss?"

"Please, Sergeant. I think we've wasted enough time around here as it is, and Mr Lawrence is clearly not going to give us any pertinent information in these surroundings, so we might as well take him in for questioning."

Lorne punched her phone, again pretending to call for backup.

Lawrence fidgeted in the doorway, his nerves showing by the sweat beading on his forehead.

"You're not doing yourself any favours, Mr Lawrence."

"I've got nothing to tell you other than I visited Bob at his request."

"Why?"

He shrugged and then leaned against the doorframe once more. Sighing, he replied, "Because he needed a mate to talk to. We all get days like that, don't we?"

"It was his choice to remain in a single cell during his sentence. Are you telling me he's complaining that he's lonely?"

"You can put that spin on it if you want to."

"So how did the conversation go?" Sally prompted. She was tired of trying to worm the truth out of him.

"That's between me and him and no concern of yours."

"Ah, but it is. As I've stated numerous times already, your visit coincides with a dead body showing up on our patch with the same MO as the victims Wallace was convicted for."

"Tough shit. That has nothing to do with me."

Sally's eyes narrowed. "The problem is, Mr Lawrence, I don't believe you."

He shrugged and pushed away from the doorframe again to raise his palms upwards. "So what? I know what you're up to. The trouble with you lot is you're so frigging transparent."

"Go on," Sally said.

"You're trying to fit me up for something I ain't done. I ain't gonna fall for it. If you ain't got any proof placing me at the crime scene, I suggest you put your detective skills to use elsewhere, because they're not working 'round here."

"Maybe that will change once the ART show up and ask you to accompany them to the station."

Nonchalantly, he shook his head. "They can try. I believe you need to have a reason for arresting me, and without any evidence at your disposal, I'd say you're up shit creek, wouldn't you? And another thing, don't think you can pull the wool over my eyes, she didn't ring for backup. Do you really think I'd be dumb enough to believe that crap?"

"Okay, we're going to give you one last chance to tell us how the conversation went between you and Wallace."

"You forgot to mention the *or*... last chance to tell us *or*..."

"I didn't, I can assure you. Time is running out, Mr Lawrence, what's it to be?"

"Your time or someone else's?" He laughed. A wicked twinkle appeared in his grey, soulless eyes.

"What's that supposed to mean?" Sally challenged, incensed.

He laughed. "That's for me to know and you to find out. Now, if we're done here, I have things I need to be getting on with."

He went to close the door, but Sally jammed her foot sideways in the gap.

"You'd be wise not to mess with me, Lawrence."

"Think you're a tough bird with your two pals standing behind ya, don't ya? Bring it on. Come back when you've got something worth talking to me about, this conversation is over. Either you remove your foot or you're going to end up in hospital getting it set in plaster, the choice, as they say, is yours," he said, his final words mimicking the way she'd said them during their conversation.

Sally relented and withdrew her foot. He sneered and slammed the door in their faces. Rather than hold a conversation within earshot of the man's front door, they descended the stairs quickly and returned to their cars.

The three of them ripped off their masks and sucked in a lungful of fresh air.

"Bastard, he knows we haven't got anything on him." Sally slammed her hand on the top of her bonnet.

"He doesn't, not really. I think he was toying with you as much as you were with him," Lorne said. She stared back at the building, her gaze rising to the second floor. "He's up there now, laughing at us, the gormless shit."

Sally turned, and there he was, in all his glory, with a pint of beer raised in front of him.

"Cheers, Inspector. Nice speaking with you. No sign of the ART yet. Tut-tut, not good, is it? Let you down a lot, do they? Can't rely on no one, not these days, eh?" He laughed and stepped away from the concrete balcony.

"Fucking prick. What an arsehole. I'm determined to nail his arse," Sally muttered through gritted teeth.

"What are you going to do now? I thought we were going to take him in for questioning," Helen said.

"Our hands are tied, we can't do that without any evidence available to us," Sally admitted.

"I've got a suggestion to make." Lorne turned her back on the building to give Sally and Helen her full attention.

"I'm all ears," Sally said.

"I think we should put him under surveillance. There's an obvious connection with Wallace, even if we can't pin the last murder on him."

Sally shrugged. "I can't help thinking that Lawrence is the type to run rings around us. If he spots us watching him, he's going to go all out to make us suffer."

Helen nodded. "While I agree with your conjecture, I

think Lorne is right. What's the alternative? I can't see one, can you?"

Sally raised her hands in front of her. "Okay, you win. We'll get Jordan and Stuart out here. Make the call, will you, Lorne? I'm not leaving this place until they arrive. We'll meet them around the corner, somewhere out of sight, otherwise he'll think he's got the upper hand over us."

JORDAN AND STUART were eager to get in on the act and joined them less than ten minutes later. Sally pointed out the flat belonging to Lawrence, and she'd already sourced an image of the man from his Facebook page that he hadn't kept up to date.

"I need you to stay out of sight. The last thing we need is him cottoning on that you're on his tail. You could be in for a long night; you'd better notify your partners. We can hang around for half an hour, keep an eye on Lawrence if you want to source some food and drink for yourselves to keep you going."

"That'd be great, boss. I noticed there was a Co-op around the corner," Jordan said.

Sally noted how good it was to see him back to his usual enthusiastic self. "Off you go, make it snappy."

The two men ran back to their car, and Stuart drove off.

"And what about us?" Helen said.

Sally picked up on her disappointment and kicked herself. "Damn, you didn't want to be on surveillance? I should have asked."

Helen frantically shook her head. "Good God, no way. My days of sitting on boring stakeouts are long gone. No, I was just wondering what we should do next, that's all."

"We'll go back to the station, follow up on any leads the team have uncovered, and that'll be us for the day. Jordan

COULD IT BE HIM?

and Stuart know they can call me day or night if there is any movement with Lawrence. There's no point all of us being out here."

"I agree. I might go back to my office, if it's okay with you? The chief is bound to want me to give her an update upon my return."

"Suits me. I'll have the rest of my emails and post to go through as it is. We'll take a detour on the way back, stop by the lab and give them the necessary kick up the backside."

"This is the frustrating lull in an investigation that we all have to deal with from time to time," Helen said. "I'll touch base with you before I leave for the day."

"Make sure you do. I'll let you know if anything happens with Lawrence."

Helen smiled, jogged back to her car and drove off.

Stuart drew up beside Sally's car.

She lowered her window and repeated what she expected of them. "No matter what time it is, if he moves, I want to hear about it, got that?"

"Absolutely, boss. We've bought enough food to feed a scout group camping out in the woods for the weekend, so there's no need to worry about us."

"I'll give you a call later before I head home. Stay alert at all times, if he sets off, make sure he doesn't clock you following him."

"Message received and understood."

"Stay safe, we're all aware how dodgy this neighbourhood can be."

AT AROUND FOUR THAT AFTERNOON, Sally received a call from Jordan, informing her that Lawrence was on the move. He was on foot and visited the Co-op, but he did meet up with a younger man. They chatted for a few minutes whilst having a cigarette.

Jordan said it wasn't a casual meeting, he got the impression that they knew each other well. They parted and went their separate ways ten minutes later, and Lawrence returned to his flat."

Sally relayed the news to Lorne and the rest of the team.

"I wonder who the young man was," Lorne said.

"If only there were CCTV cameras working in that area. I know from what's gone on in the past that no sooner are they repaired than they're attacked again by thugs."

Lorne shook her head. "Not an easy situation to deal with."

"Let's see how it pans out. If they've met once, we can't rule out them meeting again. We'll get Jordan and Stuart to keep an eye on things, and next time, maybe we'll shoot over there and have a chat with him."

"Sounds like a good idea. I'll have a look through Lawrence's friends' list on social media, see if this young man shows up."

Sally nodded. She paced the floor, unsure where to turn next.

"Hey, are you okay?" Lorne asked.

"Frustrated beyond words. My gut is telling me Lawrence has something to do with the latest murder, but he seems a crafty shit to me. He had an answer for everything today, giving me the impression that he was expecting us."

Lorne tilted her head from side to side. "Possibly, it was hard to tell. However, I do agree that he came across feistier than someone who was innocent, if that makes sense."

"It does. Let me know what you find. I'm going to keep calling the lab. I didn't appreciate being fobbed off when we dropped by earlier. How the hell are we supposed to solve the investigation if the techs down at the lab are dragging their feet?"

"Staff shortages. If I hear that excuse one more time, I

think I'll scream. Our profession has been under the cosh for years, meaning every officer I've ever worked with has had to work harder and smarter, without the need to blame cutbacks."

"Yep, we've been the same around here. It seems to be the done thing these days. I'm going to let Helen know about Lawrence, then I think we'll call it a day."

"It's been a long, frustrating day, but what's new?" Lorne laughed.

Even though Sally was eager to get home to see how Simon was, she was dreading it at the same time.

"Are you sure you're okay?" Lorne asked on their journey home.

"I'm not sure, I'll tell you when I get home and have a word with Simon. I suppose I'm apprehensive, you?"

"I was going to say the same. Why don't you take me to yours and I can go home the back way, through the gate? I'd rather be with you in case…"

"God, don't. I've been tempted to ring him all day, but then it would slip my mind. I don't want him to think I'm worried about him, you know, distracted at work. He'd go nuts if he thought that was happening."

"I think Tony would be the same."

Sally indicated and pulled into her drive. She drew up alongside Simon's Rover. "No extra damage done from what I can see."

"That's a relief."

She glanced up. The front door was open, and Simon was standing on the doorstep, holding Dex by the collar. As soon as Sally switched off the engine, he let Dex go. He was beside the car in breakneck speed. Sally opened the door, and he jumped up to lick her.

"Hello, boy, did you have a nice day with Grandma?"

"I bet your mum really missed him. He'd be company for her, too, while your dad is at work."

"Yeah, she adores him, we all do. I keep thinking what could have happened to him and it makes my blood boil."

"He's fine. Look at him, I told you he'd be okay. Trust me, dogs are pretty resilient."

"I know. I should listen to you more often."

Lorne laughed. "Yes, you should. Right, everything is obviously all okay here. I've changed my mind, I think I'll go home the long way, I fancy a bit of a walk to clear my head. Have a good evening, Sal."

"You too, hon."

Dex ran around the car as soon as Lorne opened her door. She made a quick fuss of him and then gently pushed him away, back towards the house. "Go see Daddy."

He bounded towards Simon and sat beside him.

"He's a good boy. See you at the normal time tomorrow?" Lorne was already ten feet from the car.

"Same time. Have a good one."

Lorne waved and left the drive a few seconds later. Sally turned her attention to Simon, who was smiling in the doorway.

"Hello, you. Have you had a better day today?"

"Yes, and you worry too much. I hope I did the right thing, picking Dex up from your mum's?"

"Absolutely. To be honest with you, I forgot all about him. Shame on me."

"I'm sure your mum would have rung you if I hadn't stopped by. How was your day?"

"Frustrating, I'll tell you about it later. Just to warn you, we might get disturbed this evening."

"Oh, any particular reason?"

"Two of my team are on surveillance, they've got their eye on a potential suspect."

"Hey, that's great news. I'm about to knock up a stir-fry. You can tell me all about it and go over everything else that went on today while I cook the dinner."

"Over a glass of wine, of course."

"You took the words out of my mouth. I have just the bottle for such an occasion."

Sally hooked her arm around his waist, and they entered the house together with Dex bringing up the rear.

CHAPTER 8

Sally was enjoying a lovely, peaceful dream when she was suddenly alerted to her phone vibrating across the bedside table close to her head. The clock said it was five-forty-five. "Jesus, what the hell?" She answered the phone. "DI Sally Parker. This had better be good at this time of the morning."

"Sorry, Sally, it's me, Helen. We've got another one."

Sally sat upright. "What? Another body?"

"That's right."

"Old or new? I mean, is the murder of a fresh victim or are we looking at a cold case?"

Helen sucked in a deep breath before replying, "Umm… definitely not a cold case."

"Damn, Christ, my head hurts. Sorry for the awkward question. I must have been in a deep sleep. You'd better send me the address. I'll give Lorne a call, and we'll come straight to the location. Where is it?"

"Out near the abbey. I'll send you the exact location. Pauline is here already. She and her team arrived five minutes ago."

"We'll be twenty minutes tops. See you soon."

Simon stirred beside her. "Everything all right?"

"Go back to sleep. I have to start early. Can you drop Dex off at Mum's for me?"

"Yes, leave it with me. Be careful out there."

He was snoring again before she made it to the en suite. She took her phone with her and rang Lorne from there. "Hey, sorry to call so early. Helen's just rung me, she's at another murder scene."

"Bugger, that's not what we wanted. Any news from Stuart and Jordan?"

"No, nothing. Maybe we were wrong about Lawrence after all. We'll chew that over on the way. I'll pick you up in ten minutes, if that's all right?"

"I should be ready by then. All my chores have been done in the kennels. I'm on my way back to the house."

"Okay, see you soon."

Sally ran the water and had a quick shower. She didn't wash her hair because she wouldn't have time to dry it. Ten minutes later, she was sitting outside Lorne's house, revving her engine impatiently.

"Sorry to keep you. I had to give Tony his instructions before I could leave the house."

"Lucky Tony. How is he?"

"He was fidgety during the night. I think his leg must be playing him up, although he will never admit it. Stubborn as a mule when it comes to that stump of his."

"He needs to get it sorted in case it gets infected."

"I know. I think I'll make an appointment with the doctor later and just tell him to attend. Much better than waiting around for him to make one. Where are we going? And what do you know about the vic?"

"To the abbey, and that's as much as I know. I was still half asleep when Helen rang me."

"What if we're wrong about Lawrence?"

"I'll be livid if we are. I was hoping he would slip up and we'd catch him in the act."

"I don't suppose you've had a chance to call the boys, have you?"

"No, can you check in with them, see what they have to say?"

Lorne placed the call and put it on speaker. "Jordan, it's Lorne. I'm with the boss, we're en route to another murder scene. Any news overnight from your end?"

"What? Shit! No, we've both been keeping a careful eye out for Lawrence. He hasn't left the building, not since his trip to the shop."

"Okay, thanks. We'll fill you in later. Keep your eyes open, just in case."

"We will. I swear, we haven't dropped off, either of us," Jordan was quick to add.

"It's fine. Don't fret. Speak later."

"Poor sod sounded really upset about it."

"I think I would feel the same way if I had the chief suspect under surveillance and another murder occurred. Let's hope they manage to find some evidence at the scene to either dismiss Lawrence or place him at the location. There's a possibility he might have given the boys the slip. His flat is only on the second floor, it's not that far up. If he caught them watching him, he could have shimmied down the back of the property and slipped away from them that way," Lorne said.

"I hope you're wrong, otherwise Jordan and Stuart are going to be mortified if you're right."

HELEN RAN towards them the second Sally pulled up next to

the SOCO van. She yanked open Sally's door. "I'm so glad you're here."

"Calm down. What's wrong?"

Tears brimmed in Helen's eyes and caught Sally off-guard. "It's the same killer, the bloody same MO."

"Shit!" Sally and Lorne said in unison.

"What's Pauline saying about it?" Sally asked.

"She hasn't said much up until now. She looks exhausted. She told me she didn't finish her last PM until after midnight last night."

"Damn, she needs to get some help, she can't run the department on her own, it's not practical. It's going to take its toll on her sooner or later, it has to."

"Whilst I agree, there's nothing we can do about it," Helen said. "It's not like we can jump in, ease her burden by lending her a hand, can we?"

"No, but the techs can make things easier for her," Sally pointed out. "I'll see if I can have a private word with one of them later. Do we know who the victim is?"

"Yes, Pauline found his driving licence in his wallet. There was a bank card in there as well, confirming his ID. He's Dale Gill. He lives a few streets away from the town centre. His body was found by the large bins around the back of the abbey, by an old homeless guy. He refused to hang around in case he got into trouble. That's what he told the operator."

"Fair enough. So, his hand and foot are both missing. Any sign of the limbs nearby?" Sally asked.

"Not that we've found so far. He was also attacked by a long blade. Pauline believes it was probably a machete, judging by his injuries."

Sally scanned the area. "There's a camera over there. It might be too far away to have picked up the actual murder, but it can probably give us a clue about a possible suspect."

"I spotted that earlier, too, and have already requested the footage," Helen confirmed.

"Let's hope it highlights the killer and we can track him down. Let's see what Pauline has to say. We'll get ready and meet you over there." Sally walked back to the car and opened her boot.

She handed a plastic bag to Lorne, and they slipped their respective suits on.

"Take these with you." She gave Lorne a pair of boot protectors to complete her ensemble.

They made their way to the crime scene, pausing a few feet away to cover their shoes.

"Lovely to see you, ladies. I don't suppose any of us are fully awake yet, so hang fire on the questions for a while, if you don't mind."

"Sure." Sally took a step forward to assess the victim's injuries and again glanced around her. "Was he killed here?"

Pauline was crouched next to the body. She didn't bother answering the question, not immediately. "I think it was more likely that he was dragged here, judging by the scuff marks we found a few feet away."

"So, he was on foot, and what, received a whack to the head to knock him unconscious?"

"Yes, it would appear so. There's evidence of a wound to the back of the head and plenty of blood to back up your theory. That's enough questions. Let me get on with my work."

"Okay, I can take a hint. We'll get out of your hair, for now."

"That's a relief."

The three of them wandered to the opening, and Sally again appraised the area.

"So, what are we looking at here, a random attack or was he being followed?"

Lorne shrugged. "Who knows? We need to find out if anyone was waiting for him at home. Do we know how long he's been dead?"

"Pauline thought the attack must have happened at around ten last night, judging by the rigor," Helen said.

"I can't see us getting much more out of Pauline, can you?" Sally asked.

Helen shook her head. "No. What are you suggesting?"

"That one of us stays here and the other two visit his address in case someone is at home. Do we know if anyone rang the station last night to report him missing?"

"No, I haven't got around to checking on it. I don't mind staying here, I can call the station when you've gone."

"Okay, you ready for this, Lorne? We'll drop by the house. If there's no one there, we'll come back but won't come near the scene again. I'd rather not put Pauline under further pressure."

Helen nodded and searched inside her Tyvek ensemble for her phone. Sally and Lorne left her to it, stripped off their suits at the cordon and deposited them in the black sack.

"Well, that was a waste of time putting those on," Sally grumbled.

"Not really. You're just tired and in a negative mood."

"Am I?" Sally sighed. "Maybe I am. I got the impression that we were in the way. Didn't you?"

"Hard to say. All I saw was Pauline with her head down assessing the crime scene and the injuries the victim had sustained. I think you're reading far too much into it."

"Whatever. I'm sure we're leaving the scene in capable hands. Helen seems on the ball today."

Lorne narrowed her eyes. "Is that what's getting to you?"

Sally entered the car, and once they were both settled, she said, "Not at all. She's better than she thinks she is, but she needs to have more confidence in her ability."

"She's young, she'll get there, with the right guidance. I'm sure she's picked up a great deal from working alongside us the last couple of days."

"I hope so. Maybe our babysitting days are finally over." Sally started the engine and drew away. "Remind me of the address, will you?"

"I have it on the map. Take a left at the top and then the first right, and we weren't babysitting her. Don't let her hear you say that either, she'd be mortified."

"I'm not daft." Sally fell quiet to mull over the crime scene.

If Lawrence isn't the killer, then who is? What about this mysterious young man he was seen speaking with? What if Lawrence passed on certain information to him and he carried out the attack?

"Are you going to tell me what's going on in that mind of yours?" Lorne asked.

"The usual, trying to come up with an explanation as to why someone would kill another person."

Her partner tutted. "Why don't I believe you?"

"Because you know me so well. No, in all seriousness, I was considering the possibility of Lawrence having an accomplice. What do you think? I'm still convinced he's part of this."

"I agree. Do you think this younger man might have been persuaded to kill the victim to take the heat off Lawrence?"

"That's a definite possibility in my mind. We need to find out who the younger man is."

"What about the surveillance team? They're going to need a break soon."

"That crossed my mind, too. Knowing Jordan and Stuart, they'll want to stick with Lawrence. I think I would if I were in their shoes."

"Yeah, you're right. You're going to need to give them the option, though."

"I'll sort that out after we've visited the victim's home. Was it right here?"

Lorne consulted the map on her phone. "Yes, that's it. Number twenty-six."

Sally travelled the length of the road. "I can't find it."

"Go back. There were a few houses tucked away halfway down on my side, maybe it was one of them."

Lorne was right. They exited the car and knocked on the door of the small semi-detached home, but there was no answer.

"We're going to need to wake up the neighbours," Sally said.

Lorne cringed. "We should get away with it, but only just. It's coming up to seven-thirty now."

Sally held up her crossed fingers. "May the force be with us. I'll go left, you go right." She knocked on the neighbour's front door and had her warrant card in her hand ready to show the homeowner in case they kicked off.

A woman holding a small child came to the door. "Can I help you?"

"Sorry to disturb you so early. I'm making enquiries about Dale Gill who lives next door."

"I know him. Has he done something wrong?"

"No. Does he live alone?"

"Yes. His wife walked out on him a few years ago. I haven't seen her since."

"I don't suppose you happen to know where he works, do you?"

"Let me think, he's just changed jobs, he told me that the other week. I can't remember where he told me he was working now. Have you got a card? I'm up to my eyes in getting the other kids ready for school. I'll have a think about it and get back to you later if anything comes to mind."

Sally handed the young woman a card. "What's your name?"

"Rose Nyland. Sorry, I have to go now."

"I understand. Thanks for your help."

Sally waited for Lorne to finish her conversation with the other neighbour before moving on to the next house. "Anything? Rose at number thirty said Dale had recently changed jobs."

"Yes, Mrs Falstaff said the same. She told me he worked for a design company in town. She saw him yesterday morning; he told her that he'd enrolled in a book-keeping course at the college. She thinks he was there last night."

Sally nodded. "That makes sense. He attended the college and was walking home when he got attacked. Maybe the murderer followed him from the college."

"Or attended the class with him?"

"Possibly. We should stop off at the college, but I doubt if anyone will be there at this time of the day, except for the cleaners."

Lorne's stomach rumbled. She held her hand over it. "I don't suppose we could kill some time by stopping off somewhere for breakfast, could we?"

"Why not? I think I know a little place around the corner from here. Whether it will be open at this time is another matter."

THE CAFÉ HAD OPENED its doors barely five minutes before they arrived, and the owner or waitress was still tearing around getting the upturned chairs off the tables.

"Come in, come in. Pick a table and I'll get it organised for you."

"Don't worry about us, we'll sit here." Sally chose the

closest table to the door which had already been arranged to welcome customers.

"If you're sure. I'll get you a menu." The tiny woman scampered behind the counter and brought them a laminated menu. "Here you go, unless you already know what you want?"

"I'll have a bacon roll and a flat white coffee," Lorne said, not bothering to check the menu.

"And I'll have the same," Sally replied. She handed the menu back to the waitress.

"It won't be long." The waitress shuffled off again and began noisily removing pots and pans from the draining board.

"What do you think of it all?" Lorne asked.

"I can't shift the idea that Lawrence has something to do with the murders. My biggest concern is that the lab aren't being as forthcoming as they usually are."

Lorne's mouth twisted. "Do you think that has something to do with Pauline being under pressure?"

The waitress brought them their coffees which paused their conversation. "Enjoy." She smiled and backed away.

"Where were we?" Sally asked. "Ah, yes, going back to Pauline. Let's say I'm not that enamoured with how the investigation is proceeding so far."

"In fairness to the team, they've had to deal with a cold case as well as two current cases. Looking at things from their perspective, that can't be easy."

Sally sighed, and her gaze drifted out of the window at the people in business suits going off to their offices. "I know. None of this is easy. If it was, we would have put the investigation to bed by now. Did you get in touch with Stuart and Jordan?"

"I did. They assured me they're good for another few

hours. Prepared to follow Lawrence in case he meets up with that youngster again."

"Who could he be?" Sally returned her attention to Lorne.

"I don't know. Maybe someone they're grooming between them?"

"Who they plucked off the streets?"

"Your guess is as good as mine. We won't know if it's the same person until we can view the footage."

The waitress delivered their bacon rolls with another beaming smile. "Can I get you any sauce?"

"Ketchup for both of us, thank you," Sally replied.

The waitress rushed away and returned with four sachets on a small, patterned plate. "Enjoy. I'd better get this place ready for the onslaught. I'm by myself today, my assistant rang in sick earlier, hence me being behind with the preparations."

"You're doing a great job," Sally assured her.

"I hope you haven't been put off visiting us in the future, it's not usually this chaotic."

"No chance. The food and coffee are both great," Sally responded.

Through a mouthful of bacon roll, Lorne nodded. "Yes, it's fab."

"I'll leave you to it."

Their conversation dried up until they had both satisfied their grumbling stomachs.

"Ready?" Sally downed the remains of her coffee and stood.

"Eat and run. I thought days like that were behind me."

"Sorry."

Lorne nudged her arm once they got to the front door. "I was teasing. Thanks, it was lovely. We'll definitely be back. Hopefully we won't be in such a rush next time," Lorne said to the waitress.

"And I'll be less harassed, too. Have a good day."

"We'll try." Sally approached the counter and paid the bill. "Almost ran off without paying. I don't make a habit of it, I promise."

The waitress smiled. "I believe you."

Sally left a tip in the jar and followed Lorne out of the café. "Shall we chance our arm now and try the college?"

"I think we should."

When they got there, the receptionist was sympathetic to their cause and offered as much help as they needed. Sally asked her to search the system for Dale Gill's name to see at what time his course had finished.

The receptionist put on her specs and typed a few words on her keyboard. "Ah, here we are. His course started at seven and finished at nine-thirty. Do you want to speak with his lecturer?"

"Are they here?"

"Yes, Miss Page isn't usually here at this time of the day, but she had a staff meeting to attend to at eight this morning."

"If it's not too much trouble, we promise not to keep her long. We'd also like to see someone from your security department before we leave, too, if you don't mind?"

"I can organise that for you. Let me get a meeting with Miss Page lined up for you first."

Heels clip-clopped on the marble floor behind them.

"Ah, Miss Page. I was about to ring you."

"Yes, Anna? How can I help?" The slim brunette took four paces towards them.

"These two officers would like a quiet word with you, if you can spare them a moment?"

"I have ten minutes free, will that do?" Miss Page asked Sally.

"That'd be great. Is there anywhere we can talk privately?"

Anna obliged once more and pointed to a door over on the left. "That room is free until nine."

"Thanks, Anna." Miss Page led the way.

Once inside the classroom, Miss Page stood near the front desk. "How can I help?"

"We're conducting an inquiry and would like to know if Dale Gill attended a book-keeping class with you yesterday?"

Miss Page frowned. "Why, yes, he did. There were six other students in attendance. May I ask why you want to know?"

"I'm afraid I have some bad news about Dale. His body was found this morning behind the abbey."

Miss Page gasped. "You're kidding me? He's dead?" She pulled out the nearest chair and dropped into it.

"Yes, we believe he was murdered on the way home from college, at around ten o'clock. Can you tell us if your class finished on time?"

"Umm... no, it ran over by about ten minutes. I have a lot of enthusiastic students, eager to learn. Dale was top of the class in that respect." She shook her head, somewhat shaken by the news. "He was such a friendly chap as well."

"Can you tell us if there were any signs of problems during the class? Did he get on with the other students?"

"No, it was a really interesting session last night. It was one of those lessons where we got a lot covered because I didn't have to go over things half a dozen times for one particular student who didn't understand something. And no, I don't think there were any problems with the others. I've never had any issues with that group of people. Can I ask how he died?"

"We believe he might have been struck on the back of the head, knocked unconscious and dragged down an alley. I can't go into further details as to the cause of death, sorry."

"Oh my, that poor man. He was so kind and gentle. Well

liked amongst the others. Inquisitive, always the student to ask the right question at the appropriate time. I shall miss him. It's good for a student to challenge their tutors, and he definitely did that."

"Do you know anything personal about him?" Sally asked, touched by how much the tutor was shaken up about the news.

"Only that his wife left him. He went off the rails about it, took time off from the course for a few weeks but came back more determined than ever to succeed."

"I see. But he's been okay since that happened? No down days?"

"Not that I could tell. The more we discuss this the more trouble I'm having believing that he is dead. Do you have any idea who would do this?"

"Not at the moment, hence the need to interview the people who saw him last night. Did you see him leave the grounds?"

"No, I stayed behind to clear up the room after the students had gone for the evening. I did happen to glance out of the window as he was walking through the gates."

"Ah, okay. Was he with anyone else?"

"No, he was alone."

"Can you recall anyone following him?"

Miss Page blew out a breath. "I can't say I can but I wasn't really watching out for anything untoward going on. I continued tidying up the room and left about five minutes later."

"I don't suppose you drove past him on your way home?"

She smiled, nodded and briefly closed her eyes. "Yes, as it happened, I did. Oh no, now that you've mentioned it, yes, there was someone wearing a hoodie, walking several feet behind him. I didn't take any notice of it at the time, but it's there, stuck in my memory. You don't think that was the person who killed him, do you?"

Sally sighed and perched on the desk behind her. "There's a distinct possibility. Can you tell us where you were at the time?"

"On the edge of town, just leaving it. We both lived out the same way, went the same route past the abbey." She covered her face with her hands and sobbed.

Sally gave her a few minutes.

"I'm sorry, the guilt has just washed over me. If only I had given him a lift home last night, he'd still be alive today, wouldn't he?"

"You mustn't blame yourself. Did you often give him a lift home?"

"Not every week, only once or twice."

"Did he seem any different to you during the lesson last night?"

"No, he was his usual cheerful, enthusiastic self."

"Okay, we'll leave it there for now. Can we have your phone number? We'll need a statement from you, if that's all right? Someone from the station will be in touch with you over the next few days."

"Of course it is. I won't be able to tell you anything else, though."

"We just need it on record that you might have seen someone following him."

"I understand. I'm prepared to do anything I can to assist you."

Sally held out a hand. Miss Page shook it.

"Thanks for seeing us today. Sorry it was under such sad circumstances. Here's my card. If you either think of, or hear anything, that we should know about, please don't hesitate to get in touch."

"I hope you catch whoever did this. Good people are snatched away from us all too often."

"We're going to do our best to find the person responsible. Thanks for your time."

Sally and Lorne left the room. Sally peered over her shoulder and saw Miss Page covering her face with her hands, her shoulders jiggling as she sobbed.

On the way back to the reception desk, Sally whispered, "Do you think there was more to it?"

"What? More than a tutor-student relationship?"

"Yes."

"Hard to say. Maybe we'll give her the benefit of the doubt for now."

A security guard appeared behind the reception desk.

Anna smiled. "This is Harry. I've asked him to help with your requirements."

"Thanks, that's great," Sally said.

"Walk this way, ladies. My security room is around the corner. We'll see what we can find for you, if anything."

When they reached the room, he'd already cued up the recording, and they could see all the students who had attended classes that evening, filing out through the college gates. There was a lull which Harry whizzed through before another couple of students left.

Lorne pointed at the screen. "That's him, I recognise the clothing he was wearing."

"I agree. Is it possible to keep the recording going? We're trying to see if Mr Gill was followed by someone from the college." Unfortunately, no one else appeared. "Would it be possible for you to give us a copy of the recording?"

"I can action that for you now. Can I ask what this is about? They call me Nosy Harry for a reason."

Sally smiled at the man she guessed to be nearing retirement age. "Sadly, the young man in question lost his life last night. We're heading up a murder inquiry."

"Holy sh... sorry, I nearly swore, stopped myself just in time. I've had a few conversations with Dale, he was really nice. Do you have a suspect in mind? Have you caught anyone?"

"Not yet, which is why we need all the evidence we can lay our hands on."

"Let me sort that out for you. Do you want to wait in reception while I do it? I can bring it out to you."

"We'll do that. Thanks for your help, Harry."

"My pleasure. Poor bloke, he had his whole life ahead of him—well, compared to me, he did. Life can be so harsh at times, can't it?"

"It certainly can. Will you be long? Time is marching on, and we have other people we need to interview." They didn't, but Sally knew it wouldn't do any harm to gee the man up a little.

"Be with you in two shakes of a lamb's tail."

They left him to it and paced the reception area until he rejoined them a few minutes later. He held out a disc, and Sally took it.

"It's all on there. Good luck with your investigation, ladies."

"Thanks for all your help, Harry."

Sally and Lorne left the college. They were on their way back to the car when Sally's phone rang in her pocket.

She removed it and answered it. "DI Sally Parker, how can I help?"

"It's Stuart, boss. Just letting you know that Lawrence has left his flat. We're following him at a safe distance now."

"Are you on foot?"

"Yes, Jordan is in the car. We thought it best, in case he meets up with the lad again."

"Okay, we've finished here. We'll join you. Keep in touch with your progress."

"I will."

Sally ended the call. "This could be the break we've been looking for."

They raced back to the car, and Sally pressed down hard on the accelerator to get to Lawrence's address. Lorne was ready to call Stuart once they were within a few streets of the suspect's flat.

"Not far now. Make the call, Lorne."

Lorne prodded a number and put the phone on speaker. "Hi, Stu, it's Lorne. We're coming up to Lawrence's gaff now. Where are you?"

"Two streets away. Go to the end of his estate, take the first right into Stanley Road and the next left into Comer Road. Lawrence is at the top. Looks like he's waiting for someone to show up."

"We'll be with you shortly. Hold back until we get there."

"Roger that. Do you want to leave the line open?"

"Yes, do that."

Sally put her foot down, her adrenaline playing havoc with her insides. "Let's hope we can catch the buggers."

Lorne pointed out Jordan in the car, and they pulled up behind him. Up ahead, Sally saw Stuart ducking down behind cars with Lawrence in his sights and fifty feet ahead of him.

"He definitely seems anxious to me."

"Yeah, I think you're right." Sally scanned the area but failed to see anyone else around. "I can't see anyone, can you?"

"Not yet. Maybe Lawrence is early or the person he is meeting is running late. Hang on... who's that?"

In the distance, a young man wearing a dark sweatshirt

with a hood was nervously glancing over his shoulder while he walked towards Lawrence.

"Can you see him, Stuart?" Sally asked.

"Yes, I've got him, boss."

"Hold back until he gets closer," Sally warned.

Lawrence was agitated, his arms flapping, urging the young man to get a move on.

"Wait, wait…" Sally advised again.

The two finally met, and Sally shouted, "Go, go, go."

Jordan's tyres squealed, immediately alerting Lawrence and the younger man. They both took off in opposite directions.

"Stick with the youngster, Jordan. Sod Lawrence, we can deal with him later."

Jordan tore down the street, swerving as the oncoming traffic refused to give way to him. "Tosser, get out of my way."

In the meantime, Stuart ran across the grassy verge in hot pursuit of the absconding youngster.

Then the worst thing possible happened. Jordan rammed another car, and Sally was stuck behind him. All hell broke loose with the driver Jordan had hit. Sally leapt out of the vehicle and flashed her warrant card in the hope that she could calm things down.

Stuart kept up the chase for the assailant but declared he'd lost him a few minutes later.

Sally returned to the car and thumped her thighs with her fists. "Shit, just when I thought we were getting somewhere."

"It doesn't matter. Is Jordan okay?"

"A slight bump to the head. He's insisting it's nothing."

A defeated Stuart joined them. "Sorry, boss. He was too quick for me. Jumped a high wall, and I lost him on the other side."

"Don't worry, we all did our best. Do you want to stay

with Jordan? Sort the accident out and then go home and get some rest."

"Thanks, we'll do that. What about Lawrence?"

"Leave him to us. We'll shoot back there now and have it out with him. If he kicks off, we'll call for backup."

"Sorry to have let you down."

"Hush now, you haven't."

Sally reversed the car into someone's driveway and headed back towards Lawrence's flat. "Can you see him?"

Lorne craned her neck. "Not yet. He should be in view by now, unless he's taken a detour to avoid us questioning him."

"More than likely. Shit, we were that close." Sally slammed the heel of her hand against the steering wheel.

"All right, Sal, you're going to need to calm down."

"I know. I'm sorry. Bugger, what else could we have done to have caught them?"

"Nothing. Stop punishing yourself, there will be other opportunities for us to grab them."

Sally drew the car to a halt in the same spot they parked before when they'd come to question Lawrence. "Will there? I don't think I have as much confidence as you. We were inches from them. They'll have realised that and will do everything to make sure that doesn't happen in the future."

"We're craftier than they are. Christ, think about it, hon, if you and I were criminals planning someone's murder, would we meet up in the open like they did?"

Sally grunted and left the vehicle. Lorne joined her, and they both masked up before they climbed the steps to the smelly building once more.

"Which begs the question, what if we're wrong about this?" Sally asked. "What if they're innocent and were simply meeting up as friends?"

Lorne raised her eyebrows. "Seriously? Then why did they run? Innocent people tend to stand their ground; they chose to take off. I haven't changed my mind about this, Sal, they're guilty as sin. Maybe that's been their intention all along, to toy with us. Perhaps that's the thrill they're getting out of this. Maybe they enjoy a game of cat and mouse."

"Christ, I hope not. What if they're planning on killing more people as part of their wicked game? And all the time that warped bastard is sitting in his cell, rubbing his hands together and laughing at us."

"Let him. We can't worry about that. All we can do is our best with what is put in front of us. Stop doubting yourself and let's get up there, see what he has to say for himself."

They ascended the stairs quickly, and Sally knocked on the door to Lawrence's flat. But, as expected, he didn't answer the door.

She took a step back towards the balcony and surveyed the area. "I can't see him."

Lorne shrugged. "He knows we'd come looking for him, he's not stupid. He'll be out there somewhere, watching us."

"Yeah, probably. What are we going to do?" Sally said, her heart sinking.

"I'll tell you what we're *not* going to do, give up. Let's go back to the station and thrash out a strategy for what we need to do next."

Sally sighed and nodded. "Okay, you win. Should we pull Helen in, keep her involved or go it alone?"

"Let's keep her out of it for now."

"On your head be it."

They descended the stairs again, keeping a watchful eye out for Lawrence just in case, and then returned to the station. They met up with Stuart and Jordan in the station's car park.

"What are you doing here?" Sally asked.

"We exchanged details with the driver, we're going to let the insurance companies sort it out. The car still works, but

I'll see if there's a spare one knocking around. We discussed going home, boss, but neither of us was willing to do it. We'd regret not being involved during this late stage."

Pride overrode all the other emotions pulling at Sally's strings. She gave them both a brief hug. "If we're going to solve this investigation, we do it together, the way we've always done things around here." She pushed away from them and held her nose. "But you guys need to freshen up in the gents' before you join the rest of the team."

"Consider it done, boss," Jordan said.

He and Stuart ran ahead of them.

Lorne linked arms with Sally. "One of the proudest moments of your year, eh?"

"Decade you mean. They're good lads."

THE TEAM DID INDEED SPEND the next hour or so thrashing out the options left open to them. In the end it was decided that the key remained with Bob Wallace in prison. Sally rang Governor Pike and went over their dilemma.

"Damn, that's tough on you and your team. You have my sincere apologies, Sally. But how can I help?"

"What I need to know is whether Wallace has had any other visitors while he's been inside. I don't mean recently; you've already told us that Lawrence started visiting him a few weeks ago. I know we're probably clutching at straws here, so any assistance you can give us will be a huge help."

"Okay, let me have a word with my staff and see what we can come up with to help you out. I can't promise that I'll get back to you today, I have an important meeting to attend in Norwich at four, but I will certainly do my utmost to get back to you if I'm able to."

"That would be amazing, thanks so much, Ken. Whatever information you can give us will be appreciated."

"Leave it with me. I'll get back to you as soon as I can."

Sally ended the call feeling far more positive than she'd felt all day. She shared the news with the team. Helen entered the room as soon as Sally had finished.

"Hey, how's it going?"

Helen poured herself a coffee. She seemed down in the mouth. "It's not. I can't believe I hung around at the crime scene all this time, waiting for a clue or evidence to come my way. Absolutely nothing. Pauline was the proverbial pain in the arse, tutting every time I dared to move or step in her way. In the end, I gave up. It was either that or bloody belt her one."

"I sensed she was under severe pressure, that's why we left the scene. Let's give her some space for now." Sally then brought Helen up to speed on what had happened since they had left her that morning.

"Crap, I'm not blaming you guys, but that could have been the investigation done and dusted if you'd caught the pair of them." Helen cringed when she saw the look on Sally's face and mumbled, "Sorry, that was stating the obvious, wasn't it?"

"Just a touch. I'll let you off, though. We're waiting for Ken Pike to get back to us from the prison now. I think we're in for a very long day. Let's combat that, folks, by digging through Lawrence's past via whatever means possible. We also need to trace a next of kin for the latest victim, Dale Gill. Maybe we can do that through his ex-wife. I know it's not ideal, but that's all we've got for now."

Unfortunately, Gill's ex-wife was nowhere to be found. Sally assumed she had remarried or relocated to another county. Their hands were tied now regarding the next of kin. She decided to pass the buck and let Helen do the necessary research to find any of his living relatives. In the meantime, Sally and the team would concentrate their efforts on digging up dirt on Lawrence and trying to find out who the mysterious young man was.

Their shift ended without the expected call from Ken Pike which frustrated the hell out of Sally. On the drive home, Lorne picked up on the fact that Sally was absorbed in her thoughts.

"Are you annoyed?"

Eyes wide, Sally turned to her partner and said, "What gives you that idea?"

Lorne groaned. "Come on, things happen during the course of the day that can change people's plans. Ken doesn't come across to me as the type of man who would let another professional down on purpose."

"I know. I suppose on top of the other frustrating elements we've had to deal with since our dawn start, him not getting back to me was the icing on top of a three-tiered cake."

"I get that. Hopefully he'll make amends tomorrow."

Sally forced the stale air from her lungs. "Let's hope so. It's the knowing that Lawrence has something to do with the crimes, but not having anything on him to nail his arse to the wall, that's getting to me."

Lorne rubbed Sally's arm. "Stick with it. We'll get the bastard when the time is right. Don't let the frustration overwhelm you, stop you from thinking straight or coming up with another solution for outing Lawrence."

"You're right. I promise I'll be a good girl from now on."

Sally dropped Lorne off at her gate and continued home. She entered the drive and found Simon playing fetch with Dex on the front lawn. She slowed down to a snail's pace in case Dex ran in front of the car when he laid eyes on her.

Simon called Dex to him once he spotted her vehicle. She parked up next to her husband's Rover and switched off the engine. Sally opened the door, and Dex was the first to greet her.

"Hello, boy. Have you had a good day?"

He barked excitedly and turned his back on her, eager for Simon to throw the ball for him again.

"Hey, that's enough, champ. Come on, inside, let's get your dinner sorted out."

"Does that invitation include me?" Sally asked. She fluttered her eyelashes at him.

He swept in for a kiss. "Of course it does. You look tired. How was your day, or shouldn't I ask?"

"It could have been better. One day I'd rather forget, if you don't mind?"

He hugged her and planted tender kisses all over her face until she was giggling like a teenager. "Why don't we order a takeaway for tonight and have a snuggle in front of one of those B movies we detest on Netflix?"

Sally snorted. "I think I'd rather slit my throat than have to contend with the second part of that suggestion."

"Yeah, not one of the brightest ideas I've had this week. Chinese or Indian?"

"Surprise me. Enough about me, how are things going with Jack?"

"We think he's making progress. There hasn't been an auction since the one where this guy caused trouble, but I know Jack has been following the bugger. I think he's going to make a move on him soon, once Jack's got enough proof in his locker that he's dodgy and up to no good."

"I hope he's being careful. We don't want any further trouble."

"He is, don't worry. Both Tony and I have told him the same."

It started to rain, so they ran for cover before they got soaked.

"You get changed, and I'll ring the Indian. I fancy a curry that will take me to the edge and back."

Sally laughed. "I've heard it all now. As long as I don't have to suffer the consequences in bed later with you shouting *burglar*, getting me to hide under the quilt and you letting one rip."

"What? I think you have me mixed up with one of your other fellas. I'd never dream of doing anything so offensive."

Sally ran over to the window and peered up at the sky. "There's a beauty, a big fat pink one with a huge snout flying past now."

He laughed until tears formed in his eyes. "You're nuts, what are you?"

"I must be to put up with you and your windy bum after an Indian and, on that note, I'll run upstairs and get changed."

"You should. I think you've hurt my feelings enough for one night and you've only been home five minutes."

Sally poked her tongue out at him, and Dex chased her up the stairs. She played hide-and-seek with her four-legged companion for a couple of minutes, changed out of her work clothes and returned downstairs to find her phone ringing on the worktop. "You could have answered it for me."

"What? And be in your bad books for a second time in as many minutes?"

She tutted and answered the call. "DI Sally Parker, how can I help?"

"Sally, it's Ken. I'm hoping you'll be able to forgive me for not getting back to you as promised."

"Hi, Ken. You sound harassed, is everything all right?"

"Nope, I've had one of the worst days possible."

"Oh, may I ask why?"

"Revolting prisoners."

"Aren't they all?" Sally chuckled, the tension easing in her shoulders now that he'd called.

"Not all of them, and I meant literally. A certain section of the prison began rioting, complaining that some of their rights had been stripped, and that was it for the rest of the day. I had to cancel my important meeting and act as chief negotiator until things got back to normal at around six this evening. I must reiterate, I'm sorry to have let you down."

"It's okay. We all have days when something major strikes and puts a kybosh on what we had planned. I hope no one was hurt in the riot?"

"Thankfully, no."

"Did you get very far with my request before the riot started?"

"Sadly not. I'm going to make it a priority in the morning, you have my word on that. I just wanted to touch base with you this evening to let you know I hadn't forgotten about you."

"Umm… would it be all right if my partner and I visit you in the morning? Will it be safe?"

"Yes, the prisoners were happy with the outcome to their action. Why not? Give me until ten to sort things out for you, how's that?"

"Sounds great to me, as long as I'm not putting you under pressure?"

"You're not. I apologise for interrupting your evening, please enjoy the rest of it."

"You didn't, and I will. We've just ordered a takeaway; it's been a long, frustrating day. I'll fill you in tomorrow."

"Sorry to hear that. I look forward to seeing you, Sally."

"Me, too. Take care, Ken." She ended the call and pulled out one of the chairs at the table.

"Did I hear right? There was some kind of riot at the prison today?"

Sally nodded, lost in her thoughts. "I can't help wondering if it was done on purpose."

"Surely not. Why would you believe that?" Simon handed her a glass of red wine he'd poured.

"Because of how close we came to catching Lawrence and who appears to be his associate today. Oh, I don't know, perhaps I'm talking nonsense because I'm tired and irritable."

"You, irritable? Never." He took a step towards her, pulled her to her feet, and they shared a hug. "Why don't we brush work aside for the rest of the evening and have some us time for a change?"

"You always say the right thing at the right time. I'm up for that."

CHAPTER 9

"Thanks for agreeing to see us again at short notice, Ken. I hope you're having a better day than yesterday, so far?"

"Always a pleasure to see you both, and yes, it's all quiet around here today. I've got a surprise for you."

Sally took a seat in his office and inclined her head. "Tell me more."

Lorne sat next to her with her notebook and pen at the ready.

"I felt so bad about letting you down yesterday that I came in early today to ensure I personally gathered all the information you requested."

She saw a mischievous sparkle in his eye, and Sally's heart skipped several beats. "You really didn't have to do that and, for the record, you didn't let me down. Something happened that was out of your control. Although, I do have one question about the situation that took place here yesterday."

"And what's that?"

"Can you tell me if Bob Wallace was involved in the riot?"

"Funny you should say that, he was the instigator. Why do you ask?"

Sally informed him about where their investigation had led them the day before.

"Jesus, what the hell is going on around here?" Ken asked. "Forget I asked, it was rhetorical, I think we're all aware of what we're up against. Why don't you come with me to the security room, and I'll show you, rather than tell you, what I've discovered?"

"Lead the way," Sally replied.

The three of them walked down the long corridor that didn't go anywhere near the prisoners, which was a relief to Sally. It was always there, in the back of her mind, that she might bump into Darryl during a visit.

There was an officer already in the room.

Ken introduced them. "Terry, these are DI Sally Parker and DS Lorne Warner. Terry is the expert with all this equipment. Have you got the footage lined up for us?"

Terry smiled at Sally and Lorne and then faced his equipment. On the screen was the reception area where Sally and Lorne had come through earlier. "I think this is the youngster arriving here." He froze the frame and pressed a button. The printer to the right of him churned into life and spewed out a copy of the photo. Terry handed the piece of paper to Sally.

She studied it and passed it to Lorne who regarded it through narrowed eyes. "It could be him. I'm not sure we got a close enough look at him. We could compare it to the other images we have of the youngster when we get back to the station."

"That's what I was thinking," Sally agreed. "Do you know who he is?"

Ken nodded. "He's been to visit Bob Wallace a few times over the past year. It's his son."

Sally and Lorne stared at each other.

"Damn, we weren't even aware that he had one," Sally admitted.

"I'm not surprised. He goes under a different name. I asked around, and one of the guards got chatting to him when he first started visiting. The young man let it slip that he'd just turned eighteen and had gained access to his adoption file which led him to Bob Wallace."

Sally slapped a hand over her mouth and shook her head. She dropped her hand and whispered, "If this is true, it's unbelievable. So, what are we saying here, that his father is manipulating him to go on a killing spree? Making the boy prove that he's his flesh and blood?"

"It's a shocking possibility," Lorne said.

"Damn, I hadn't even thought about that," Ken admitted. "We've got more footage to show you."

The screen changed to the room where the prisoners were allowed to meet their families. The youngster entered the room nervously and took his place at one of the tables. Wallace came in and stood opposite him for a while, as if sizing the youngster up, before he eventually sat opposite him.

"Shit, the young man, sorry, do we know his name?" Sally asked.

"According to the name he signed in with and who the visiting order is made out to, it's Wayne Bradley."

Sally nodded. "What I was going to say is, Wayne is giving the impression that he's in awe of Wallace."

"You're right," Lorne said. "Oh God, it's sickening to watch."

"There's more footage, unless you've seen enough?" Ken asked.

"I think we've seen enough, but I have a favour to ask of both of you."

COULD IT BE HIM?

"And what's that?" Ken asked, grinning.

"Can we get a copy of the footage from all of his visits?"

"Already sorted for you. This is your copy we're viewing, isn't it, Terry?"

"That's right, Governor."

"You say the visiting orders are sent out. Does that mean you have an address for Wayne?"

Ken winked and pointed a finger. "I wondered when the penny would drop." He handed her a sheet of paper. On it was an address that would lead them back to Wymondham.

"It's not too far from where Lawrence lives." Sally handed the sheet to Lorne who agreed with a brief nod.

"Well, this has turned out to be an extremely fruitful trip. I had my doubts if it would be. I can't thank you enough for putting all of this together for us, Ken."

"I hope it helps and that it puts a stop to all the killings."

"You're not the only one. What an evil bastard Wallace must be to manipulate his son in this way, and Lawrence, he must still be part of this."

"I totally agree. I'll show you out, ladies."

Terry ejected the disc, slotted it into a plastic case and handed it to Lorne as they left the room.

THEY DROVE BACK to the station rather than go straight to Wayne Bradley's address. Sally was eager to do some extra research on the young man before they showed up at his home to arrest him.

"Maybe we should put him under surveillance," Lorne suggested.

Sally contemplated the option for a while. Helen had joined them upon their arrival. She had been as shocked as they were to learn the news about Bradley.

"I think that would be the answer," Helen said. "We can't

take the risk of letting him roam free in case he decides to kill someone else."

Sally turned to Stuart and Jordan to gauge their reaction. They both jumped out of their seats and hitched on their jackets.

"We're up for it, boss," Jordan said, his enthusiasm evident.

"Okay, you get out there, same instructions as yesterday: stay out of view and follow him if he leaves the house. We'll do the necessary research on him while you're out there."

"We'll let you know if he moves," Jordan said.

He and Stuart tore out of the room as if they had hot coals under their feet.

"Right, let's get cracking, see what we can find out about Bradley, or should we call him Master Wallace now? No, we'll stick with Bradley."

Lorne drew Sally's attention and pointed to her computer screen. "I've got his Facebook page and Instagram accounts up; they both make interesting reading."

Sally used the mouse beside Lorne to scroll through Wayne's accounts. There were pictures of Bob Wallace everywhere, and the words 'my hero' written next to his photo. Sally shuddered. "This is gross. How could he be that twisted to believe his real father is a hero? Can we go back to what his social media accounts were like before he met up with Bob Wallace?"

Lorne scrolled back to ten months prior and beyond. "This is when things changed. Before then he didn't really have much to say for himself. Most of what he posted, up to meeting his father again, were gloomy at best. Everything was flipped on its head when he announced that he had found out he was adopted and that he'd tracked down his father."

"Sick bugger, he's definitely got his real father's genes. What do we know about his adoptive parents, anything?"

Lorne went through Wayne's friends' list on Facebook. "Mother is Elizabeth and father is Frank. Ah, here's something interesting. The father died a few months before Wayne's eighteenth birthday."

Sally groaned. "That was the trigger point to get in touch with Wallace, once he came of age then. Christ, I bet that broke his adoptive mother's heart. I don't suppose it's on there, but I wonder how long he was with the family. How many years ago was he given up for adoption? What happened to his real mother? Christ, I could go on. Let's work hard, folks, concentrate all our efforts on finding out the details behind the adoption. How did his adoptive father die? Is his adoptive mother still with us?"

"We're on it," Lorne replied. "Joanna, can you get in touch with the adoption people for me? Helen, can you call the birth, deaths and marriages department?"

Both colleagues gave Lorne the thumbs-up.

Knowing that everything was being taken care of, Sally slipped into her office to go through the mind-numbing paperwork on her desk. Throughout the chore, she was distracted and put most of the correspondence that needed a response to one side, not wishing to get bogged down in case she was needed elsewhere.

Lorne interrupted her half an hour later. "Are you free to chat?"

"Come in. What have you found out?"

Lorne sat and sighed. "His real mother, Yvonne, died of breast cancer when she was married to Bob Wallace at the time. He couldn't cope with the child so put him in the care system. I checked Wallace's record when he was arrested, and it stated that he was on antidepressants."

"He was depressed after she died and so put his kid into care?"

"So it would seem. Wayne was three at the time. I suppose a child of that age can be a bit of a handful."

"I wouldn't know. At what age was Wayne adopted by the Bradleys?"

"When he was six."

Sally tapped her pen. "So, he spent three years in the care system? And what about his adoptive mother, is she still with us?"

"As far as we can tell."

"Okay, I'm almost finished here. Is there anything else we need to check, or do you think we've covered it all now?"

"I'm going to keep trawling through his SM accounts, see if there's anything else showing up on there."

"Can you specifically look at his more recent activity? What he wrote on his pages after victims two and three had died?"

"Leave it with me."

No sooner had Lorne left the room than Sally's mobile rang. "Lorne, this could be the boys, get ready to make a move. Warn Helen as well."

Lorne gave her a thumbs-up from the doorway.

Sally answered the call. "Stuart, what's going on?"

"We're following Bradley at present, boss. Just checking in with you to let you know. He's on foot."

"Okay, any idea where he's going? Towards Lawrence's flat or not?"

"No, he's heading in the opposite direction."

"Keep me informed." She ended the call and left her office. "It was a false alarm, maybe. He's on the move, however, Stuart says he's going in the opposite direction to where he met up with Lawrence yesterday."

"Maybe he's running an errand for his mum," Lorne suggested.

"We'll soon find out. I'm in desperate need of a coffee, anyone else want one?"

She ended up making drinks for all of them and then paced the floor while she drank her coffee until her mobile rang again. "What's going on, Stuart?"

"He ended up going to the newsagent's, picked up a paper and some milk and walked home again."

"Did he spot you?"

"No, we made sure we kept out of view this time, boss. What do you want us to do?"

"Stick with him. It's still early. He didn't meet up with Lawrence until later in the day yesterday, so let's not dismiss the possibility of them meeting up again just yet. Bearing in mind two murders have happened this week already."

"Got it, boss. We'll sit tight and keep you informed."

Sally ended the call and ran a hand around her face. "Am I the only one sensing that this is going to go tits up?"

Lorne laughed. "Chill, the boys have got him covered. Here's something interesting we've been working on while you've been slaving away over your mind-numbing chore in your office."

"What's that?"

"We've been studying the images we have of the murderer and comparing them to Wayne Bradley's height and build from the clips taken during his visits at the prison, and there's no doubt in our minds that they're a match."

"Great, will that theory stand up in court, though? We'll pass it on to the CPS and leave it up to them to decide, if we ever arrest the bastard."

"We will. Where's your PMA gone?" Lorne chastised her.

"It's upped and left me at the moment. I hate all this hanging around, twiddling my fingers."

Lorne laughed. "Speak for yourself. The rest of us have made a lot of headway this morning."

"I know, it was a figure of speech," Sally stated. "Joanna, do you fancy nipping out to the baker's?"

"I don't mind. I could do with some fresh air; I've got a headache from hell today."

Sally did the rounds, jotting down on a sheet of scrap paper what sandwich everyone preferred.

Joanna left and returned with the bagful of goodies twenty minutes later and declared, "I know it wasn't on the list of requirements, but I bought a packet of doughnuts for us to share as well, my treat."

"Thanks, Joanna, how's your head?"

"A little better."

WITH LUNCH out of the way it was back to pacing the floor for Sally. That was until five o'clock struck and her mobile rang. She'd been willing it to ring for almost two hours but still jumped when it sprang into life. "Stuart? Any news for us?"

"Yes, boss. He's on the move again. He's setting off at a fast speed. He's got a rucksack with him this time, so this feels different."

"Okay, we're going to join you. I'll keep the line open. Helen, Lorne, this is it."

The three of them gathered their coats and left the office with Joanna's good luck wishes ringing in their ears.

"I'm going to sign out a Taser," Sally said. She threw her car keys to Lorne and dashed through the door to the armoury, where she signed out the Taser and then left the building to join Lorne and Helen. "Stuart, are you still there?"

"Yes, boss."

"We're on the way to your location now. Once I'm in the car I'll put you on speaker. Is he still on foot?"

"He is."

"Okay, I'm at the car now." Sally slid behind the steering wheel and slotted her phone in the holder on the dashboard. She drove to the location Lorne had already entered into the satnav. "Almost there, Stuart, where are you?"

"He's just passing the school two streets from his home. What's the name of the road, Jordan?"

"Tyler Street."

Lorne ran her finger over the map and tapped it. "Turn left at the next junction, the school should be on the right at the top."

"Got it. We'll follow you Stuart and, depending on how far he travels or if he gets an inkling he's being followed, we'll swap positions. Just let us know."

"Will do."

Lorne pointed ahead. "There's Stuart's car."

"Right, we're coming up behind you now."

"We've got eyes on you."

They travelled another five minutes until Bradley ran down an alley. "Damn, I think he's spotted us. He's legged it."

"Can you go ahead, try and cut him off? We'll stay this end in case he decides to run back."

"Put your foot down, Jordan," Stuart instructed his partner.

Sally drew the car to a halt in a nearby parking space, and the three of them exited the car and ran up the alley. At the top they had two choices, left or right.

"Shit, which way?"

Lorne craned her neck. A dog barked, and then what sounded like a bin tipping over came from the left.

"I'm taking a chance it's this way." Lorne led the way, followed by Helen, and Sally brought up the rear. Lorne soon tired, and Sally and Helen caught up with her. "He's up ahead."

Sally upped her pace and rounded the corner. She caught sight of Bradley disappearing into a garden. "Shit. Lorne, hold back. Ring Stuart and Jordan, tell them he's entered a garden down the alley. We're going to need backup." She sensed he was about to take the homeowner hostage, if they were at home.

"I'm on it," Lorne called back breathlessly.

"Helen, come with me. Are you up for this?"

"I'm with you all the way, Sal. Just tell me what you want me to do."

"Follow my lead, but most of all keep safe. I'll fire my Taser at the first opportunity rather than put anyone at risk."

Helen nodded, and they ran to the open gate to find Bradley banging on the back door of a semi-detached house. A woman on the inside screamed at him to leave her alone.

"Wayne Bradley, turn around slowly to face me. I'm armed, don't try anything you might later regret."

He kicked out at a pot plant on his right and faced them.

"Drop your bag on the floor," Sally ordered.

"Or what? You ain't got the guts to fire that thing, lady, I can see your hands shaking. You're shit-scared because you know what I'm capable of."

Sally had a clear shot, and rather than get into a debate with him, she fired. Footsteps sounded behind her. Stuart and Jordan entered the garden and ran towards Bradley. Sally released her finger, and her colleagues removed the wires from Bradley's chest and placed cuffs on him.

He was dazed when he was pulled to his feet, but that didn't stop him kicking out at Stuart and Jordan.

"Behave, or we'll deck you," Jordan warned.

Bradley spat in Jordan's face.

"You bastard!" Jordan hooked his leg in front of Bradley, and he ended up face-first on the ground.

Stuart removed a spare mask from his pocket and attempted to put it on Bradley in case he spat at them again. He twisted his head, making it difficult for Stuart to cover his mouth and nose. Mission accomplished, they got Bradley to his feet again and marched him past Sally and Helen and out of the garden.

Helen unexpectedly gave Sally a hug. "You're my hero."

Lorne laughed from the gateway. "She's been mine for years."

Sally swiped her hand in front of her. "Get outta here. Well, that was easier than expected. I'm glad the woman had the sense not to open her door to him, otherwise it could have been a different outcome entirely. I'd better check she's all right and let her know what just happened."

BACK AT THE STATION, as it was approaching six-thirty, Sally dismissed the rest of the team. Lorne insisted staying behind to assist with the interview. They had to wait another twenty minutes before the duty solicitor arrived. Wayne Bradley attended the interview under duress. He was anything but quiet. A male officer was forced to stand behind his chair throughout. Not that Bradley said much. With every question Sally asked, he either grinned or sneered and uttered the two words that most guilty prisoners said: "No comment."

Eventually, after ninety minutes of trying to get a single response out of him, Sally called an end to the interview. "Okay, we'll play it your way and try again in the morning. Maybe a night in a cell, like your father, will change your mind."

"I doubt it. Bring it on, bitch. You ain't getting nothing out of me, full stop!"

"We'll see about that. Maybe we'll pick your accomplice Mr Lawrence up, see if he'll talk now he knows that you're banged up."

"Do what you like. We're smarter than you dumb coppers."

Sally grinned at him and said, "Define smart for me? Because I think your definition and mine are worlds apart. Surely if you were that smart you wouldn't have got caught today and you wouldn't be sleeping in a police cell overnight, would you?"

He suddenly shot forward. But the officer behind Bradley grabbed him by the shoulders and pulled him back.

"Not a wise move, Mr Bradley," the duty solicitor, Miss Fletcher, said.

"Fuck off, who asked for your opinion?"

Miss Fletcher stood and walked towards the door. "I can see I'm no longer needed here."

"Thank you for your time, Miss Fletcher. Will you be back in the morning?" Sally stood and approached the woman.

"I don't think so. I'll pass the case over to a male colleague, if that's okay with you? They'll be more suited to Mr Bradley's needs."

"I agree." Sally returned to the table and spoke to the constable. "Take him back to his cell. Do you need a hand?"

"No, I'm sure Mr Bradley won't think about causing any trouble, will you, son?"

Bradley grinned and shrugged. "Depends, and I ain't your son."

"Thank God for that," the constable responded and escorted Bradley back to his cell.

Sally and Lorne followed them, just in case the youngster kicked off. He didn't. Maybe Sally's words had the required impact after all.

COULD IT BE HIM?

. . .

WHEN SALLY ARRIVED home that night, after another long day, she found there was an extra car sitting in the drive, one that she didn't recognise. "Oh crap, this doesn't look good. What the fuck is going on?" She kicked herself for signing her Taser back in before she'd left the station. She ran up the steps to the manor house and eased the door open. Two male voices could be heard in the lounge. She gently closed the door behind her and crept along the hallway. The voices dulled instead of getting louder.

After the day she'd had, she shouted, "I know you're in there. I've got a weapon and I'm not afraid to use it." She burst into the room to find Simon sitting on one end of the sofa and Jack on the other. "Crap, I thought there was... never mind, how are you, Jack?"

"I'd normally say very well, but my ex-boss has just threatened me with an invisible weapon so I'm a teeny bit concerned about her mental state right now."

Sally roared with laughter and collapsed onto the sofa between them. "Let's just say it's been one of those days."

"Ah, the important question is, did you capture the criminal?" Jack said jovially.

"We did, before he could harm anyone else. Enough about my work, how are you getting on with your project?"

"Jack has made great progress," Simon said. "Sorry, I should let him fill you in."

Sally held Simon's hand and squeezed it. "I don't care who tells me, just give me the details."

"Well, this guy Steve Groome, has got a lot of properties on the go in the area. I followed him for a couple of days when he visited the sites. He's very pally with his workers, but I also saw a nasty side to the moron today."

"In what way?" Sally asked.

"He showed up at one site, found two guys messing around, flinging bags of cement to each other until one of them split, making a right mess. They didn't see their boss arrive, and let's just say they're going to regret not being more alert in the future. Groome always goes from site to site with a musclebound goon on hand. This guy laid into the two jokers and one of them ended up going to hospital with a broken arm and the other one ran off before he could really take a beating."

"Oh shit. What about this guy's background? Any idea where he's getting his money from to buy all these properties? If he's got a fair few being renovated at present, that's going to be a pretty penny he has tied up at any one time."

"Yep, I've asked around on the quiet, and word has it that a few years ago he was in the drugs game. Never got caught, he was too careful for that. He soon realised there was money to be had renovating properties and now employs most of the builders, dodgy or otherwise, in the area."

"And what does he do with the properties once they're completed?"

"The larger ones he tends to sell on at a vast profit, but the smaller ones, I'm talking anything smaller than four beds, he rents out."

"Shit, can you imagine what it would be like renting from him and the punishment he would mete out to anyone who failed to pay their rent one day?"

"Exactly," Jack said.

"Okay, so where do we go from here?" Simon asked.

"If he's a heavyweight criminal then you guys need to be careful. Why don't you give me any evidence you've uncovered so far and I'll pass it on to the Fraud Squad? I know a guy over there who owes me a favour or two. I'm sure they'll be interested in the fact his dirty money originated from drug dealing. Maybe some of it still does if he's got that many projects on the go at the same time."

"Sounds like a plan," Jack agreed. "Even though I hate handing the reins over to someone else when I've spent the last few days putting in all the groundwork."

Sally pinched his cheek. "Diddums, you'll get over it. Are you stopping for something to eat? I'm starving."

"I'd better be on my way. Donna was expecting me home a couple of hours ago, but I wanted to bring you guys up to date on what I'd found before I called it a day. So, if you'll excuse me, I'll be on my way."

Simon and Sally showed him to the front door.

"I'll make the call first thing and get back to you. Get all the evidence to me as soon as you can, Jack. Let's hope we can bring this bugger down without anyone getting hurt."

"We'll see." Jack waved and walked over to his car.

Simon closed the door and wrapped his arms around Sally's waist. "Congratulations on nailing the bugger."

"Thanks, he went down the 'no comment' route when Lorne and I questioned him earlier, but I think a night in the cells will make him change his mind."

"Christ, really? That's optimistic of you."

"Let's hope I'm right. What's for dinner?"

"I knocked up a cottage pie earlier. I was halfway through preparing the veg when Jack showed up."

"Do you need a hand?"

"No, you get changed, dinner won't be too long. I put it in the oven on low, I'll just turn it up and finish off doing the veg."

Sally kissed him. "I know when I'm not wanted. I won't be long." She ran up the stairs with Dex at her heels. She stopped to give him some fuss once they were in the bedroom then jumped in the shower and changed into her leisure suit. Before she went back downstairs, she called Neil Morgan, who worked in the Fraud Squad, to see what his take was on everything Jack had uncovered.

"Hey, Sal, long time no hear. What can I do for you?"

Sally filled in the details for him and then asked, "Is there anything you can do to help us out? This guy is making our lives hell."

"I can certainly delve into it for you. You said Jack's now a PI?"

"That's right. Between you and me, although he's gathered a lot of evidence against this guy, I'd rather not let him go any further."

"I totally get where you're coming from. This bloke sounds dangerous, and who knows what will happen if he suspects Jack's tailing him?"

"My thoughts exactly. Jack's going to bring me all the evidence in the morning. I'll drop by and see you first thing, although I won't be able to hang around for a chat as I have a serial killer to interview."

"I love the way you just dropped that snippet of information into the conversation. I'm hearing great things about you and that renowned new partner of yours. I take my hat off to you, Sally, you're both a force to be reckoned with."

"Aww… thanks, Neil. Yeah, although, to be fair, we did need a little extra help on this one. It was a joint case with DI Helen Edmonds. Do you know her?"

"I've heard the name, but the reports haven't been good. Hey, working with you two can only be an excellent prospect for her career."

"Only time will tell. I'll let you enjoy the rest of your evening now. Take care."

"See you in the morning, bright and early."

"You will."

Sally ran a brush through her hair and studied her features in the mirror. Over the last few months, she hadn't really had the chance to check out her appearance and was shocked to see how many lines were now showing. "Damn, I need to do something about that before they get any worse."

EPILOGUE

The next morning, Jack showed up at the house to drop off the evidence he had gathered. Sally stopped off to see Neil in the Fraud Squad before she joined the rest of the team.

"Right, before Lorne and I go into battle again with Bradley, Stuart and Jordan, I need you to bring Lawrence in. I think we have enough on him to arrest him for being an accessory to murder, at least."

"That should wipe that smug smile off his face," Lorne said.

"Not half," Sally agreed. "Are you ready for round two?"

"Want me to check if the duty solicitor is here yet?"

"Yep, if you would?"

Sally had a quick word with Stuart and Jordan before they left the office.

"The solicitor is already here and waiting in reception," Lorne told her.

"Okay, let's get things rolling. I'm just in the mood for Bradley today. Whether his attitude has changed overnight or not, I won't be taking it easy on him. Can you fetch the file we have on him, Lorne, it's on my desk?"

Sally downed the rest of her coffee and met Lorne at the door. "It's not ideal interviewing him after only throwing one cup of coffee down my neck, but shit happens."

Lorne laughed and continued to laugh as they descended the stairs.

"It wasn't that funny," Sally said once they'd reached the bottom.

"Think again. I was envisioning how your lack of caffeine is going to turn this interview on its head. I bet he ends up a nervous wreck."

"Look out, Bradley. He's not going to know what's hit him."

They introduced themselves to the male solicitor, Rory McKenzie, and settled in Interview Room One while they waited for Bradley to join them. As soon as he entered the room, Sally sensed the change in him. He was less feisty for a start and avoided eye contact with her.

Lorne said the necessary verbiage for the recording, and Sally began asking question after question with Bradley being super cooperative. He admitted to committing the two murders and the fact that his father, Bob Wallace, had initially put him up to the task.

"Why allow him to manipulate you like that?" Sally asked.

Bradley shrugged. "I wanted to have him in my life and thought this was a way of pleasing him."

"What? By taking two innocent men's lives? Just for the sake of it?"

"Yes, I regret my actions. I'm sorry I did it. Can I go now?"

Sally found his naivety bizarre and a little unnerving. "You think just by apologising that will be the end of it? That we're going to set you free?"

"Yes, won't it?"

Sally's eyes widened. "Definitely not. The families of the two victims would string us up if we did that. No, you're going to pay for robbing the victims of their lives. You'll be lucky if you ever see the light of day again. In fact, if I have my way, you never will. I think all this today has been a charade, with one aim in mind, to try and get a lesser sentence out of us. I'll tell you something, I've dealt with a vast assortment of suspects over the years, and you are way up there at the top for being the most manipulative. Did Daddy tell you how to behave during this interview? Or did your evil mind work it out for itself?"

His eyes narrowed, and he sneered at her. "I didn't need my father to tell me what to do, and here's another little nugget of information... just like him, I've left you a few more bodies to discover. Good luck with your search, bitch."

His admission stirred up her insides. She had trouble reading him, to know if his threat was real or not. "Take him back to his cell, Constable. This interview is over. Now we have his admission recorded, I'll pass the file over to the CPS for them to proceed with his conviction. Have a nice life, Mr Bradley, you'll be spending the rest of it in prison, alongside your real father. Both of you have proved to be a menace to our society and deserve to spend the rest of your days behind bars."

He stood and spat at her and was quickly tackled to the floor by the constable. Lorne ran to the door and called for assistance. Two more uniformed officers appeared. They pounced on Bradley, and he was escorted back to his cell.

"Are you all right?" Lorne asked.

Sally wiped the spittle from her face and shrugged. "I'll survive. The question is, will he, on the inside? I have my doubts."

"He's definitely one we should tell Ken to keep an eye on if he ends up in the same nick as his father."

. . .

LATER THAT DAY, Sally received a call from Jack.

"Sal, sorry, we're going to need backup down here. We're at the Portland Road address, and Groome is here causing trouble."

"We're on our way."

Sally shot out of her chair in the office and ordered the team to follow her. She instructed Joanna to stay behind. Sally and Jordan both signed out Tasers before they left the station.

She threw her car keys to Lorne. "You drive, I don't trust myself to get us there in one piece."

During the drive, which was frantic, left to her partner, Sally managed to get in touch with Neil and apprised him of the situation.

"I can be there in ten minutes. We've got this, Sal."

"I hope so. The last thing I want is for someone to get injured by this clown."

LORNE DREW up outside the property. Sally and Jordan took the lead and entered the front door first to find the house, which was going to be put on the market by the end of the week, had been trashed.

"Bastard, where are they?"

There was no sign of anyone downstairs. Jordan and Stuart checked upstairs and delivered the news it was all clear up there, too.

Lorne dashed into the kitchen, opened the back door and found six men in the rear garden. Jack, Simon, Tony and three other men who were threatening them with metal bars. Jack and Tony were doing their best to talk the men down, but the one who appeared to be in charge had other ideas.

Sally and Jordan raced into the garden.

"Put the weapons down or we'll fire," Sally shouted, her Taser aimed at the brute standing closest to her husband.

"What the fuck? Ignore them," the bloke in charge grunted.

"I'd listen to her if I were you, mate," Tony warned. "She's got a keen eye and a steady hand. She's never missed a target yet."

"Fuck off, it's all for show. Women don't know how to handle them things. I've never known a copper shoot one yet."

He charged at her husband, his bar aloft, and Sally fired without hesitation. The wires pierced the mouthy man's chest, and he collapsed to the ground. It looked like he was having a seizure as fifty thousand volts shot through his prostrate body. The other two men dropped the bars they were holding and held their hands above their heads.

"Don't shoot, we're unarmed."

Jordan passed his weapon to Sally. She kept it trained on the two goons, ready to fire it at either one of them if they dared to move an inch. Lorne, Stuart and Jordan attached their cuffs to the three criminals just as four officers came out of the back door behind them.

"Hey, I thought you needed help? Looks like you've handled everything on your own," Neil said. He patted Sally on the back and then fist bumped her. "Do you want us to take a couple back with us?"

"If you don't mind. Stuart and Jordan can take the other one, while Lorne and I sort out the damage here."

"Hey, Jack, how are you doing, mate?"

"I'm okay, Neil. Er... thanks for your assistance." Jack laughed.

"I hear you're finding your feet as a PI. Good on you."

"I'm getting there. I've had a few successes under my belt, although I needed my ex-boss to bail me out of this one."

"It's great to have friends in high places, eh?" Neil grinned and led his men, and the criminals, back through the house.

Lorne and Sally both hugged their husbands, and then Jack joined in with a group hug.

"Thanks, Jack, for all you've done." Sally kissed him on the cheek.

"Hey, I did nothing. I was following the fucker this morning, and as soon as they got out of the car and headed into the house, I sensed there was going to be trouble, so I got on the blower to you. Tony was in the middle of negotiating with the fuckers when I joined in the fun."

"Well, with the evidence you've collected on him, we've got enough to make him regret his bullying tactics. Why don't we call it a day and head home?"

"No can do," Simon said, "I have to stay behind and clear up the mess they made."

Sally looked at Lorne, and they both nodded.

"It'll be quicker if we all lend a hand."

Tears welled up in Simon's eyes. "I can't ask you to do that. It could take days to put right."

"We can break the back of it tonight," Sally replied.

"Hey, I'll chip in, too, for a few hours," Jack said.

Simon was overwhelmed and hugged all of them again. "Teamwork makes the dream work, eh? You guys are the best."

THE END

Thank you for reading Could it be Him? The next book in this exciting cold case series **Frozen In Time** is now available.

In the meantime, have you read any of my other fast paced crime thrillers yet? Why not try the first book in the DI Sara Ramsey series No Right to Kill

Or grab the first book in the bestselling, award-winning, Justice series here, Cruel Justice.

Or the first book in the spin-off Justice Again series, Gone In Seconds.

Why not try the first book in the DI Sam Cobbs series, set in the beautiful Lake District, To Die For.

Perhaps you'd prefer to try one of my other police procedural series, the DI Kayli Bright series which begins with The Missing Children.

Or maybe you'd enjoy the DI Sally Parker series set in Norfolk, Wrong Place.

Or my gritty police procedural starring DI Nelson set in Manchester, Torn Apart.

. . .

COULD IT BE HIM?

Or maybe you'd like to try one of my successful psychological thrillers <u>She's Gone</u>, <u>I KNOW THE TRUTH</u> or <u>Shattered Lives.</u>

KEEP IN TOUCH WITH M A COMLEY

Pick up a FREE novella by signing up to my newsletter today.
https://BookHip.com/WBRTGW

BookBub
www.bookbub.com/authors/m-a-comley

Blog

http://melcomley.blogspot.com

Why not join my special Facebook group to take part in monthly giveaways.

Readers' Group

Printed in Dunstable, United Kingdom